HER LOVER

—·—

INSPIRED ROMANCE

SINMISOLA OGÚNYINKA

Cover Concept by Baseline Creatives © 2019

Author Photo by Babstudio © 2014

PWG PUBLISHING

LAGOS

Dedicated to my sweet sister, Adetunmbi,
and her remarkable husband, Ayodeji Ogunsoto.

HER LOVER

Inspired Romance

1

Nikky covered CJ's face with kisses and he chuckled.

"You won't let me finish up here on time to take you out." He caught her lower lip. "Choose."

"Choose what?" She moaned. "You don't have time for me." She dropped on his laps, decidedly putting herself between him and his open laptop.

"If I give time the way you want it, we'll both go hungry." He leaned forward to catch her lips, but she stood abruptly. "Oh, smart child."

She didn't reply and he shook his head, returning to his screen. He knew he worked hard and much as he tried to not bring work home, he did. Who was to blame? He was still a bachelor and sometimes he cringed at the thought of losing his freedom to a woman like Nikky. She crowded every space she occupied. But he really loved her. She remained the only woman he had ever given his house key to. And would have married her if she wasn't still in university. Howbeit, in her final year, which mattered to him because he wanted a working woman as his wife.

Nikky returned within five minutes, her bag slung over her shoulder.

He arched an eyebrow. "You just got here. Where are you going?"

"What do you care?"

She headed for his front door. CJ didn't have a lot of energy to stop her at the moment. It was Thursday and he had a presentation first thing in the morning. If he didn't finish up now, he'd be done for. Maybe it was better she left, and he'd make up later. Their make-ups were always...hmm. Perhaps he didn't mind her spontaneous anger and silly moods.

He half-stood. "Babe, wait. Let me order dinner."

She slammed the door after her. CJ smiled. "She'll soon be back."

He returned to preparing the summons for the next day in court.

****

The weekend sped by before CJ realized it was Sunday evening. The suits he filed had been thrown out of court on technicalities and his boss, well, more like the Managing Partner, a SAN, had been livid. This client had a lot at stake and was paying a huge amount to sue a multi-national company for fraud. Monies they would recover in paid damages. If, the case was won, and this made the client edgy. CJ was at fault and he blamed it on the few hours Nikky disturbed his peace on Thursday night. He should have stayed back in his office to finish up. She'd be angry but she sometimes spent the night when she visited, and he wasn't home. But it had been her birthday and he'd promised to take her out, thinking he'd be done. With the corrections made to the processes he drafted, and a new suit filed, though, only money and time was wasted, not justice.

He closed his laptop after sending a draft of the new suit and thought of what to eat. Nikky rarely cooked because he hardly ate. His slim profile testified to that.

"Where is she, anyway?" he mumbled.

He hadn't heard from her since she stomped off, which wasn't unusual. He picked his phone and dialled. Nikky's number rang to the end, twice. She did know how to keep malice with him, time he would use to make up for lost events in his life because when Nikky made-up, she took over his space. That was why their quarrels were frequent. He used the time to get his life on track. He smiled at the thought and went ahead to find a loaf of bread in his fridge. With a can of coke, he was fine for the evening. Then he sent Nikky a text message promising to pick her up the following night. She didn't respond. It occurred to him to send her a WhatsApp message instead. He would know when she read his message. And as expected, the message showed two blue ticks at once. He called again and she didn't pick up. This time, he recorded a message and blew a long kiss for effect.

"I miss you, lover-girl."

The following night, CJ closed from work early to make up and keep his promise. His girlfriend had not replied his message and had been offline all day, which was unusual. Even if she was still upset with him, she would keep her phone open. But with

Nikky, you never really knew. She could be venting and instead of letting him know she was available, switch off her phone just to frustrate him.

Nikky lived in a two-room apartment she shared with two other girls, close to her university. One room was taken by one of the girls, while she and Amanda shared a room. When CJ arrived, Amanda let him in.

"Hi." Amanda seemed breathless. "Sorry, I didn't hear your knocking."

"Hello, Amanda." CJ smiled. "Nikky home?"

"Huh, no." She scratched her neck. "She went to campus to read. She has a test coming up."

"A test?" CJ arched an eyebrow. "Is exam not starting this week?"

"No. Exam is still two weeks." Amanda swallowed. "Come in. Do you want to eat something?"

"No, thanks." He sighed. "She hasn't been online today."

"Are you sure? Maybe her phone battery died." Amanda stepped back. "Let me prepare something for you. She should soon be back."

CJ sat on one of the two chairs in the room. "Okay, thanks."

Amanda exited the room as though in a hurry. In the ten months CJ had dated Nikky, he had visited her maybe thrice. He remained cordial with her friends and nothing more. Accepting a meal from Amanda was the strangest thing he would ever do, because he wasn't the type. All his previous girlfriends' friends remained at a polite distance. He never even had time to build relationships with the girls not to talk of with their friends.

He didn't know much about this Amanda besides the fact that she shared a room with Nikky and was also a final year student at the same school. He had no idea what course she studied. Sitting with her and eating didn't seem like something he wanted to do, especially with Nikky, in class, studying for a test...He got on his feet and walked through the shared living room to the kitchen. Amanda was stirring something in a pot with one hand and holding her phone to her ear with the other, speaking rapidly. CJ cleared his throat and Amanda swung around.

"Sorry, but I need to leave."

She took the phone off without hanging up. "It's almost ready. Just porridge."

"No, I'll pass. Thanks. Let me run." He sniffed a nice aroma. "Ask Nikky to call me."

"I will," she said. "I don't know why her phone is off. I just tried it now as well."

CJ walked towards the door and she followed him. "You don't have to see me out. Thanks."

"Okay, thanks for coming."

She closed the door after him a little too loudly. CJ knew something was off with the way the girl fidgeted but he didn't figure what. Nikky could be cheating on him but that she went to read for a test was a tall story. His girlfriend didn't study for anything. She paid others to do it for her. That much he knew.

2

The cleaning lady opened the front door with the apartment key from the property managers and went about her work a few minutes before CJ arrived. He'd totally forgotten she was scheduled to come in this Saturday. Management usually sent text messages the day before, but he must have missed it. Three new cases had his attention and he had to work on them urgently. Ever since he became a partner in his law firm a year back, work had tripled when he'd thought things would slow down. He remembered the threat he'd constantly faced about not being made a partner if he didn't work so hard. Now he should relax a bit, things had just gotten tougher. Of course, now he shared profit so his remuneration had gone above the roof and he could afford a house of his own in a luxury estate.

He had opted to work from home because his study was a yard-long better than his office and for some sickening reason, Wi-Fi at the office was down. A cleaner in the house was the last thing he wanted. Besides, he had forgotten to do the necessary preliminary tidying mandated to precede the bi-weekly cleaning. The middle-aged woman sent from management office had been around for a while and he sighed with relief. A new person would be tough to convince he wasn't home for any form of chores and didn't want to be disturbed.

"*Oga*, thank God you're here." The woman turned around when he entered his house. "You forgot to clear the—"

He didn't allow her to finish her statement. "I'm sorry, but I can't do it now. I have too much work." He headed for his study. "Please, *abeg*, sorry."

The woman laughed. "Okay, sir. Please call management office to let them know."

He shut the door behind him and dropped his bag on the double couch. He didn't care about calling management. He trusted her, and if she stole from him, too bad. The air-conditioning, which he normally left on was chilly, just what he needed. He opened his laptop and got down to work. He had to appear in court on Tuesday for one of the cases and he had just discovered his argument was still in a draft form. Within minutes, his head was in his work.

"The clothes in the basket on the floor, sir. Should I take to the laundromat for you? They are women clothes."

CJ pretended he didn't hear her.

****

Amanda walked through the corridors of the Chemistry department, her heart throbbing in her chest. The deserted passage with all the offices locked left her with trepidation. This was not supposed to be happening, and she wished she could have gotten someone to come with her. But on the other hand, she'd rather face this alone. She got to the room she was going and pushed the door open. It was a small lecture room linked to the Chemistry laboratory the final year students used exclusively. The odd smells of ammonium and other pungent chemicals wafted through to her, but her gaze was fixed on the girl seated on a high stool against the wall, reading a novel.

She looked up when the door creaked. "Hi."

Amanda breathed in. "She hasn't come back."

The other girl's eyes widened. "Are you serious?"

"Will I joke about things like that?" Amanda sighed. "You said you people arrived together."

"Of course." The girl stole a glance at her novel but didn't close it. "You called her?"

"Her phone is not going through again."

"When was the last time you spoke?"

Amanda looked up, trying to calculate. "Um, her guy came on Monday. So, I think Monday, or Sunday in the middle of the night."

"Me I was back by then. We came in Sunday night." The girl turned to her novel again and acted as though Amanda was no longer there.

"Do you have the address, or a number to call?"

Her eyes widened. "*Hian*, nobody has any number. What are you saying?" Realization seemed to enter her eyes and she stood. "Is Nikky a baby? Please don't ask me questions like that again."

Amanda moaned. "But you were with her. You spoke with her when you people travelled together."

"Please, please don't tell me that. I was with her how? Am I her nanny?" She gripped her novel and moved toward the entrance.

Amanda thought she was leaving but she only peeped and came back to her seat.

"Okay, give me your name at least, and number."

The girl focused on her novel as though she was alone. Amanda had a decision to make, to leave or continue to loiter and hope the girl would talk.

"If it was you, would Nikky not have given some information to your friends and family?"

The girl hissed and stood again. This time, she left the lecture room. Amanda drew in several deep breaths. She had no idea what to do. Was she to report to school authorities Nikky left home on Friday after classes and hadn't returned in over a week? She wasn't even resident on campus. Knowing the system the school operated, the level of concern would be very minimal. Students dropped out of the university all the time and there was nothing school authorities did about it. Besides, she could have returned to her "village" as they would say.

Amanda left the room and returned to her accommodation. She didn't have CJ's contact, or she could have reached out to him. Nikky's brother's number could not connect and she was reluctant to call her mother. Why would her boyfriend not even come around again? She knew Nikky was in the relationship just for the guy's money but at least he seemed genuine. She opened the wardrobe she shared with Nikky and took her friend's clothes out one at a time, looking for anything that could give her a clue as to what to do. She knew she would not find Nikky's location amongst her belongings but there could be something else, a diary or address book with at least another sibling or cousin's number to call. She found nothing useful.

The other roommate, Alaba, hardly ever had anything more to do with her and Nikky and hadn't even asked after her. It wasn't strange. They were university students and would sometimes go weeks without seeing one another and especially as exams approached and the end of the semester drew near. But Amanda needed advice desperately. She and Nikky were the best of friends and had many other friends but she didn't want to raise an alarm only for Nikky to show up after a day, smiling from ear to ear.

Alaba was in her room eating with her hand from a deep bowl, and watching TV when Amanda knocked and entered. A half-naked man was sprawled on her bed, fast asleep, and snoring softly.

"Sorry to disturb—"

Alaba placed her index finger on her lips. "*Ssh*." She stood and led Amanda out of the room with her bowl of food.

"How far?"

"Nikky hasn't come back since she travelled last week Friday."

Alaba gasped. "Her number is not going?"

"No."

"Huh. Did you call her house?"

Amanda shook her head. "Her brother's number is not connecting, and I don't want to call her mother, you know."

"Hmm, of course." Alaba lowered her voice. "I didn't even notice. What will we do? School will not answer us and police—"

"Ah, I don't want police *wahala*." Amanda threw her hands up in the air. "You know how that is."

"*Shey* she has one boyfriend like that. The lawyer-guy."

Amanda scratched her head. "I don't have his number."

"I do." Alaba dropped her bowl on the centre table and Amanda noticed she was using her hand to sip "garri" and groundnut. "My bobo had one small problem one time and Nikky gave me his number. Let me get it."

She hurried off and returned shortly with her phone. "I just sent it to you."

Amanda sighed. "Thank you, Alaba. Let me call him."

"Okay. Let me know how it goes."

3

—·—

C J did not check his phone until close to midnight when he was sure he could sleep the whole day on Sunday, ready for his series of meetings on Monday, court appearance on Tuesday and a barrage of paperwork and consulting the rest of the week, including routine court appearance on Friday. The way the week ran by was ridiculous. As usual when he put his phone on silent and ignored it all day, he had tons of messages and missed calls but only one frantic text message got him jumping out of his bed.

"Hello, Amanda!"

"Hello, CJ." Her voice sounded strained. "I thought I got the wrong number."

"Where are you?" He checked his watch. "It's late now but I'll come first thing in the morning."

"Okay, thank you," she whimpered.

"Where are you?"

"In our house."

"See you tomorrow morning." He hung up and paced.

CJ had known something was wrong. He kicked himself for not taking note and action. It had been six days since Nikky went missing, and he hadn't missed her. He felt miserable. To think this was a girl he wanted to marry. Six days, and he had not even noticed her absence.

The following morning, he was at her apartment before 6 am. Amanda was awake already.

He barely got into her bedroom before he started speaking. "So, when was the last time you saw her?"

She looked up at the ceiling. "Friday before last. She was going to class."

"And she didn't return?" He growled. "But I came on Monday you said she went to class."

"Oh, sorry, it was Monday. She said she had a test."

CJ paced. "And she didn't return that night and you didn't think you should call anybody?"

"She's an adult. Sometimes she will go to your place. I don't use phone to chase her about."

CJ glared at her. "So why are you chasing her about now?

"Because her number wasn't going through again."

"But...anyway, so you were in touch with her on phone until yesterday when you called me?"

"No, I wasn't in touch with her. But her phone was going through. She didn't pick up." She rubbed her forehead. "Nikky is like that sometimes. She will not pick up."

"For six days? She has never been like that with me."

Amanda muttered an expletive under her breath. "Please, since that Monday, did you hear from her?"

"No."

It was Amanda's turn to be furious and she made it clear. "And you didn't even check on her. And here I was thinking she was with you."

"How about I was thinking she was here in her house, attending her classes normally, preparing for her finals?"

Her voice cracked. "Please, are you here to help or what?"

He ran his hand through his head, doing nothing to ruffle his low-cut hair. "I'm sorry. We need to get the police involved. Inform her mother too."

CJ hated to have to be the one to speak to anyone in Nikky's family. They didn't know him officially and he neither, so Amanda called Nikky's mother in Imeko, a small town widely known as the spiritual headquarters of a big church in the country. Nikky had told him her mother was an elder in the church and highly religious, fanatic. He'd concluded, unreasonable.

He asked Amanda to put the call on speaker-phone so he'd listen in. The voice on the other end sounded unexpectedly young.

"Mummy, it's Amanda. Nikky's friend."

"Ah, Amanda. How are you? How is school?"

Unexpectedly polished too, CJ thought.

"I'm fine, thanks ma." Amanda paused. "Did...I wanted to ask if Nikky arrived safely. Her number is not going through."

Nikky's mother giggled. "Arrived in spirit or in flesh?"

"She...she was supposed to come home." Amanda stammered. "Her number is not going through."

Nikky's mother paused for a second. "You know your friend. If she's going to *kontagora*, she will say it is *kotonu*. I haven't seen her. But give her a few days."

CJ couldn't believe his ears. From a mother? There was no hint of anxiety or concern.

Amanda swallowed. "Yes, ma."

"My dear, you caught me on my way to morning prayers. Let me hurry so I will not be late. Thank you for your call." She hung up before Amanda could respond.

CJ smirked. "Seriously? Did she understand you were asking after her daughter?"

"Mummy is...she is a woman of faith. Unless Nikky goes missing, she won't, you know, she won't be worried." Amanda sighed. "She will start praying about it, though."

CJ frowned. "What did she mean by Nikky going to *kontagora* and saying she's going somewhere else?"

Amanda shrugged. "What do we do now?"

He knew she was hiding something. "You lied to me that she went to class, and now lied to her mother. What do you know that I don't?"

She covered her face with both hands and shuddered. CJ wanted to jerk those hands off her face. Nikky must have been with another man or why would Amanda be so secretive. Instead of yelling as he so wished he could, he lowered his voice and spoke softly.

"We should go to the police, but they can't help if you don't tell the truth." He exhaled. "She was with me on Thursday. But I was so busy I didn't have time for her."

"It was her birthday." Amanda winced. "She told me she would spend the night with you."

CJ swallowed. The implication of her last statement did not dawn on him until he and Amanda were in front of the police detective later in the morning. Nikky had spent the night "with him" on Thursday. But that wasn't true. She had stomped out on him. So, where did she spend the night?

4

The detective asked the same question over and over again without recording or taking notes and after almost an hour told them the university police department could not take the case because Nikky did not reside on campus. Amanda had never been more frustrated. After the dreaded call to Nikky's mum, which had shocked her as much as CJ though she hid her surprise, and the continued way CJ assessed her, she just wanted all of this to go away, and to return to her room to find Nikky asleep, drunk or stoned but alive.

CJ drove to the closest police station outside of campus. The stony silence between the two made Amanda uncomfortable. She knew in her heart the police would only take a lot of money and probably do nothing but short of keeping Nikky's disappearance to herself, there was nothing else she could do, and she felt partially responsible. If the case had been opposite, she'd expect Nikky to check her out as well.

Only one police officer was at the counter when they entered the station. The officer was impatient and took details of the report.

CJ glared at the bent head of the officer who seemed to be adding his own statement in the report. "When should we expect to hear from you?"

"I cannot tell you that. Until DPO sees the case."

CJ clenched his teeth. "Which is?"

"Oga, I don't know." The officer stared back. "All these university girls will go and stay with sugar-daddy for one month and their brother will be looking for them!"

Amanda rolled her eyes. "Please, our numbers are on the report. Can you give us a call?"

The policeman snickered and assessed Amanda in a suggestive manner. "Will you give me the money for credit?"

CJ pulled out his wallet and removed four ₦500 notes. "Please call me or her. Appreciate."

"Okay." The officer tucked the money into his pocket with a simple "thank you."

"Thank you," Amanda murmured.

They left and drove out of the premises. "Do you want to eat something?" CJ said.

Amanda shrugged. "Okay, thank you."

He found a parking spot in a crowded Sweet Sensation fast food restaurant and got out of the car. Amanda's mind reeled. Maybe she should not have involved him. She had panicked and he hadn't even asked after Nikky in almost a week. She had never taken a second look at him but now she couldn't see what Nikky could have wanted in this man, besides the money, of course. But from what Amanda gathered, he hadn't spent a lot of it on Nikky. But how would she even know? Nikky was so secretive about her man...men.

She took a second look at his sleek white Mercedes, a 4-matic, and the nice shirt and outfit. He was a lawyer after all and knew how to look good. She thought he looked too good for her or Nikky.

They got into the packed restaurant and found a seat recently vacated at a corner. A waitress hurried over and cleaned the table.

"I think you should stay so we keep the space. What would you like to eat?"

Amanda took a seat and thought about it. She didn't know what to eat, didn't feel like anything.

"Meat pie."

He arched an eyebrow. "Okay. Huh, drink?"

She shrugged. "Coke."

"I'll be right back."

He walked away towards the counter and long waiting line and Amanda's gaze followed him subconsciously. He wore clothes that fitted his tall, slender figure, and had a youthful bounce she couldn't place his age. Nikky never talked a lot about her men because in their world, good men got snatched, and she had seemed keen on keeping this one for longer than the others. Amanda hadn't been in a relationship for so long, she wondered what it was like sometimes. Though, she cared little about it. There were other issues she was pre-occupied with, tops her graduation. She had roughly a month left, and wanted to make it count, end it right to give herself better chances. She couldn't afford to not finish this year. Neither Nikky, nor any of their other friends knew exactly what she was going through in her academics. One wrong grade, and she'd be truncated. After five years of studying a four-year course...

CJ returned with a full plate of savoury pastries and two bottles of coke. "I thought you may want to try other stuff." He sat. "Do you go to church?"

She shrugged, unwilling to tell him a lot about herself. "Sometimes I go with Nikky."

He took a bite off a meat pie and she followed suit. They ate quietly for a few minutes and then he tapped the table as if to get her attention. Not as though he didn't have it. She couldn't keep her eyes away from him.

"I don't. I thought you may have to be somewhere so I can plan to meet up later." He leaned forward. "But since you're not going anywhere, we can take our time."

It didn't sound personal in any way but through Amanda's eardrum into the centre of her chest, it seemed he was asking for a date. The matter-of-fact arch of his eyebrows and levelness of his gaze spoke otherwise.

"Have you met Nikky's mother before?"

"Yes. I've visited her house too."

CJ grunted. "Really? We were to go last Christmas, but I was busy. I thought we could make it at Easter." He shrugged. "That didn't work too."

"She didn't tell me about it."

"How long have you been friends?"

Amanda munched to gather her thoughts. He was a lawyer! He would ask every imaginable question and she didn't think she could endure it. She knew he had caught her lying about some things too. This wasn't funny at the moment and she would rather be somewhere else to get her next steps coordinated. Nonetheless, it would be ridiculous not to answer such harmless questions.

"A long time." She frowned. "We met in her first year."

"Four years ago." CJ nodded. "She hardly talked about you, though. Or any of her friends."

She didn't know why she became defensive, but she did. "She didn't talk about you, either."

"Interesting." He chuckled. "I thought I was important to her."

"We don't factor importance in such ways."

She knew he wanted to talk about Nikky's disappearance and trying to make light chatter frustrated her more than she wanted to admit. And the fact that she was so aware of him made her miserable. He had great teeth, and when he smiled, a little dimple appeared on his right cheek. She wasn't supposed to notice that.

"How do you factor importance?"

She frowned. "Maybe after marriage. I don't know. Fashion."

"Fashion is important."

"Yes." She shrugged. "To every woman. So, we talk about it."

He took a long drink and then leaned forward, and it seemed to her, as though for the kill.

"On Nikky's birthday, she didn't spend the night in my house." He paused for effect. "Do you know where she went?"

Her throat went dry. "No."

5

— · —

Amanda was lying again, and CJ had never seen anyone with such a transparent face. A very pretty one too. He doubted if she had said a full true sentence since he met her officially.

"You'll make a horrible witness," he mumbled. "You can't even lie without blinking."

"What do you want me to say?" She growled, taking him unawares. "She said she was coming to you. So, did she?"

"She did."

His answer seemed to surprise her, and she bit on her lower lip. "So, why do you ask me where she went?"

"She came by and left because I was busy."

"Mister busy-busy. Even on a girl's birthday." She rolled her eyes. "So, you were the last to see her then."

CJ gasped. "What do you mean by that?"

She threw her hands up. "We spoke on the phone. She left in the morning of Thursday and we only spoke over the phone."

CJ snickered. "Seriously? So, Friday morning? Talk to me."

She couldn't even hide her reluctance. After several minutes of soft grunts and light shrugs, she cleared her throat. "When

I left the room, she had not returned, which is not unusual. I called her in the evening when I got back, and she wasn't there. She said she'd be home soon." She shrugged. "And she came."

CJ grunted. "Come on, Amanda, or whatever you call yourself. Did you see her on Friday evening or not?"

She stood. "I need to get back to my house."

CJ pressed his lips together. "Why did you call me when you know where your friend is?"

"I don't know where she is. I haven't seen her since...since—"

He snapped. "Thursday, Friday or Monday?"

She drew in a sharp breath and headed for the door. There was no use following her. She had told him one thing and it was the truth. When Nikky stomped out of his house on Thursday evening, she went somewhere else and he needed to find who or where the place was. He picked his second meat pie and chewed on it thoughtfully.

As a lawyer working in a top law firm and being a partner, it was amazing the wealth of quality-people he had in his contact list. Many of them had given him jobs privately. He'd bought land, sold property, followed some around to intimidate the press or the police, done the silliest things sometimes without a fee, and now he needed to call on those favours.

It was still Sunday morning and he reckoned people would be in church or waking up late, so instead, he took the time to scout through his contacts and form a plan. Whether Amanda deliberately cooperated or not, he was going to find where Nikky was and it had nothing to do with his relationship with her. For the first time in his life, he surprised himself with this line of thought. Amanda was his reason to find Nikky, and this destroyed every sense of moral he ever had.

He called Yemi Alade sometime after lunchtime. Yemi was married to his beautiful wife, Kemi and the two had three kids. Sunday afternoon was strictly for family time. CJ knew it was also the best time to catch Yemi in his downtime.

"Hey, buddy, how far?" Yemi said in a sing-song voice. "Good news for me?"

CJ laughed. "You like money too much. I need your help."

"Sounds serious. What happened?"

CJ cleared his throat. "You're not going to like this, but I can't think of any other way."

By the time CJ finished stating his request, he could hear Yemi grabbing his car keys and shouting to Kemi he'd be back soon. They met at a bamboo bar close to Yemi's house.

CJ started speaking as they shook hands. "I know what you're thinking but what will I do? Her roommate is not talking."

A waiter walked over and took their order for drinks. Both didn't want to eat anything. The boy returned a few minutes later with two cold beers and left them alone afterward.

Yemi shook his head. "This is serious." He scratched his temple. "You know things keep changing and now to get into my office, I have to go through an automated clock in. As soon as I approach the door, I'm captured."

"Come on, is it unusual to go to the office on a Sunday afternoon?"

Yemi sighed. "It's not but it's what you want me to go and do that is unusual."

"Yeah, I get you." CJ dropped his head. "I need her phone records. How else will I be able to trace her?"

"Let's do this tomorrow morning, CJ. I'll call one of my guys in security to give me a permit."

CJ smirked. "You need a permit?"

"Yes, I do. It's a classified document. We don't trace people's calls unless there's a reason to. A security permit."

"Wow. I didn't think it would be this complicated." CJ heaved. "But you understand my dilemma, don't you?"

"Sure." Yemi took a sip of his beer. "Are you sure you don't want to pass this through police?"

"I don't plan to use it for anything public." CJ stared at the sweating bottle of beer. "She's missing, Yemi. I can't even believe it."

"Should I tell you my candid opinion?"

"She's not missing, I know. Just cheating."

"Exactly." Yemi finished his beer and dragged CJ's closer. "Kemi will kill you."

CJ laughed. "You. The death is on you, buddy, if you get drunk."

Yemi smirked. "Get drunk on two beers."

"It's happened before, lily-liver!" CJ sighed. "My only problem is with Nikky's friend. Why would she be so worried? And call me. I mean if Nikky is cheating."

"Because you came in search of Nikky." Yemi sipped the beer slower than before. "I bet the friend has a crush on you too and wants to mess with her friend. These campus girls can't be trusted. I don't even know what you went to find there."

"Nikky is...you know her. She'll do anything for a guy."

"*Onijekuje!*"

"I understand what that means, clown!" CJ joined Yemi to laugh. "I don't eat rubbish!"

"Then marry! And not a flimsy campus chick looking to milk you dry."

CJ rolled his eyes. "I don't think Amanda is like that. I mean, Nikky."

Yemi threw his head back and laughed.

6

—·—

Yemi had been boss for a long time at his communications company job but CJ felt he was putting him on the edge for the first time. Not that Yemi could complain. For five years CJ had handled all his properties in Lagos for little to nothing. Besides the fact that Yemi's company didn't know about his real estate empire, CJ continued to expand the business.

They sat in Yemi's office long after close of work on Monday and looked through the report.

"I specifically asked for Thursday to yesterday. It's easier if the days are shorter," Yemi said.

"Sure." CJ studied the printout from Thursday and realized just how much of call time Nikky indulged in. "Do you have a highlighter, please?"

"Yes." Yemi stood. "But before you paint it, let's do a photocopy."

"Great idea. Thanks."

As he did the copying, Yemi exclaimed. "Look at this list. Thursday to Monday is busy but from Tuesday morning, nothing!"

CJ dashed to his side and took the sheet from him. "She called no one, texted no one." His head shot up to Yemi. "What does this mean?"

"You tell me." He finished the copies and took it back with him to his seat. "Let's mark the photocopy. You can keep the original safe."

CJ collected it from him. "Yeah, thanks."

He couldn't help but notice the slight tremble of his hands as he clutched the sheets of paper and sat. Yemi took the last blank page from him.

"Let's start from the top." He traced the calls to the time CJ said Nikky left him. "Highlight this number." CJ did.

Nikky didn't call any strange number until the following day when there were three other numbers she called. Her last call was to Amanda in the middle of the night between Sunday and Monday, but she called two other numbers. Her last call was made in the early hours of Tuesday. CJ burned with anger at, not Nikky, but her friend who couldn't keep from lying.

"Is it possible to trace the owners of these numbers?"

Yemi swallowed. "Yes. Hmm, CJ, this thing I'm doing...I could—"

"Lose your job!" CJ laughed. "And face your real estate business squarely and continue to make millions!" CJ pointed at the paper in front of him. "Please, get these people for me. Thank you."

Yemi pushed him though he wasn't blocking his way and returned to his seat. Within minutes he pulled out the full history of the owners of the numbers Nikky called and printed them.

"This doesn't look good, CJ. I'm worried for you."

"What do you see there?" CJ walked around to stand beside him. His eyes roamed for just a second. "What? Lokoja!"

****

Amanda had just stepped out of the bathroom when her phone started ringing for the fifth time. She picked it up with wet fingers and pressed her lips together. It was the call she dreaded.

"I'm at your door," CJ said stiffly.

He didn't allow her to respond before he hung up. She threw her towel aside and dressed quickly. After all, it was close to 1am and she wasn't supposed to get unwanted visitors. She moved into her sitting room and heard Alaba and her boyfriend moaning loud enough for the whole street to hear. Amanda rolled her eyes and jerked the door open.

CJ stepped inside and his eyes went toward the door on the other side of the sitting room. Amanda saw the way his jaw twitched but he said nothing as she led him to her room. Surprising her, he took one of the two chairs in the room. He clasped his hands and when he spoke, his voice was calm. Amanda noticed he probably hadn't been to his house to freshen up all day but his white shirt, pulled at the side off his fitted trousers and the still-polished-looking black shoes, plus the heady mix of his perfume and male smell, got her a bit disoriented.

"I'm sorry to come here so late." He drew in a deep breath. "I found some things very disturbing and I thought you may be able to understand them."

She stood over him, which made her feel some form of control over her thudding heart. His presence was so compelling like he could do anything, or make her do anything. After she ran off at the fast-food restaurant, she had not had any peace of mind. His effect on her put her in the most compromised situation she could remember. Did she feel like this the last few times she met him with Nikky? She didn't think so.

"What did you find?"

He stood, shrinking the space in the room considerably. "You tell me what you know about Nikky's whereabouts."

She bit her lower lip. "Did the police contact you?"

"No." He paused. "The police did not contact me yet. But I can make them contact me right now if I want." He glared at her. "Now, answer my questions."

"If I had answers, I would not have called you to find out where my friend is."

He scratched his thin moustache, grown to join a small, manicured beard. "I'm sure you're regretting that now, because, babe, you're in deep trouble and I'm going to mess you up, big time."

With his voice so normal, his words sent a flurry of fear-waves through her. What happened to Nikky? She knew they didn't both live straight, but something must have happened, and she feared the worst. Nikky would never disappear. She had talked about settling down with this "rich, lawyer guy" after graduation. She would not just throw that away willingly!

"I don't know where Nikky is." She returned his gaze. "And yes, I regret coming to you because you have not been of any help."

She was the first to look away.

"Did her mother call back?"

"No."

"Hmm." He moved closer to the king-size bed. "Did you try her number again?"

"No."

"Who is Larry or Lanre?"

Amanda breathed hard. "Nikky's boyfriend."

7

—·—

Amanda's answer was like a punch to CJ's stomach, but he laughed instead. Right now, he knew it didn't matter at all if Nikky was missing or not. He didn't care. After he had Yemi pull up her call and text records, he couldn't be bothered about where she was. Nikky had at least two other relationships and this made CJ less responsible. According to Yemi, good riddance. But for the one person he now stood in the same room with, he felt answerable, and no justification for that either. He owed neither girl nothing. Of course, he had touted amongst his friends he wanted to marry Nikky but that as well could have been as far as any relationship could go. Ten months wasn't the longest he had been with a girl.

He tore his gaze away from Amanda. "How many boyfriends does Nikky have?"

"I don't know."

He snickered. Perhaps he should leave, forget all of this happened. That there was a Nikky and an Amanda. No one would really ask after his girlfriend. His family members who knew her would accept the relationship ended without asking why; everyone around him knew he was a very busy man and a woman who would stick around long enough to stay until forever must be very special. Yet, he couldn't leave well alone. What would he gain by pursuing this? Nothing. Except he'd have a reason to see Amanda a few more times, probably.

As soon as he walked in to her house, he knew she just had a bath and for a second, he feared she had a man with her. But she was alone. And this was when he allowed himself to sniff her fresh smell, and glance at her braless outfit. She must have quickly flung it on when he called to let her know he was around. Why would she be having a bath in the middle of the night? Maybe a man just left? Why should it bother him!

"How many of them do you know?"

She hesitated. "You. And Larry."

CJ arched an eyebrow. "Jinad?"

"I don't know him." She sighed. "Look, I know Nikky moved around but she didn't tell me about all of it. I only got to know about you and Larry because she seemed to have some future plans with you two."

CJ sneered. "Future plans with two of us. Like she's a bigamist or what?"

"Well, it's none of my—"

"I suspect. Just like your relationships is none of her business too." CJ cursed. "You live together but have little or nothing in common. You deceive yourselves, living your fake lives. Isn't that true?" CJ increasingly raised his voice, unable to stop himself. "Why are you looking for her? Does she owe you?"

"No!" She shouted back. "Please, come and start going. I'm sorry I came to you. I thought you could help but obviously."

He swung around to see her walk to the door, swaying her hips provocatively. It didn't look like she had any underwear on, and he wanted to hit his head for noticing. She opened the door and his senses disappeared for a second. He didn't stop himself because he couldn't. With a few long strides, he closed up on her, and slammed the door shut.

"Never ask me to get out!" He grabbed her upper arm. "Is that clear?"

She lowered her voice. "If you don't let go of me now, I will wound you."

CJ let go of her and moved away, breathing hard and willing himself to calm down, after all, this was supposed to be about Nikky. And he didn't care anymore. She said the words before he could.

"Now you know she was cheating, what does it matter to you anyway?"

"You may not be able to understand. You girls obviously don't have any value for commitment."

Amanda snickered. "Please, give me a break."

He flexed his fingers and took a decision. "I totally agree with you. I thought I was the only man in Nikky's life. I'm not. I will assume she got angry with me and has moved on to her other interests."

"Good decision."

He walked to the door and opened it. Goodness, he felt like a fool already.

8

Yemi called two weeks later to find out if anything came up and CJ gave him a definitive "no."

Yemi chuckled. "I just put my job on the line for no reason."

"Sorry." Both laughed.

"Has she resurfaced?"

CJ sighed. "I don't know. Not in my life though."

"Do you know, out of curiosity, I went back to her account."

Something stirred in CJ's heart. Empathy, maybe. This was a girl he was going to marry this time last month.

"She's back online?"

Yemi laughed. "You didn't even call her or text her again?"

"Talk to me, Yemi, I'm in the middle of a brief."

"As always." Yemi snickered. "Anyhow, she hasn't been online since that day, and my guess is she has dumped that line. But. Now this is very interesting."

CJ rolled his eyes at the suspense Yemi was trying to create but refused to prompt the other guy.

"She had up to five guys on you, man. Where did you meet her from? All these campus girls. I can never ever ever—"

"Ah, give me a break, Yemi. Where do you meet campus girls?"

The two laughed again. CJ's secretary, Alice, an intern, walked in.

"Hold on, Yemi please." He put the phone down. "Yes?"

Alice had a face she must imagine would fit a lawyer, serious, composed. CJ thought it made her look ten years older than whatever her age was.

"There's a young woman here to see you," Alice said. "A university student."

CJ picked his phone. "Yemi, please let me call you back. Bye."

"Sure."

CJ hung up and arched an eyebrow. This was not a good time at all, but it was close to seven, he did need to finish a brief and present it before going home. Yet, a university student, young woman, just set him off.

"She doesn't have a name?"

"Alaba."

The name didn't register at all. CJ shrugged. "I don't know her. What does she want?"

"She said she's Nikky's housemate, but you don't know her personally."

CJ sneered. "Send her in. And please, I'm sending you a draft of my brief. Review it and send back."

Alice checked her watch, which irritated CJ unending. "Okay, sir," she mumbled and left.

Closing time was five but he couldn't remember if he ever left work on time. Add five hours unless he packed the stuff and took it home to close at midnight. His thoughts drifted to the girl coming to see him. Nikky did have another housemate. Must be the one he heard the other night, having loud sex like an animal.

She walked in and CJ was surprised to see a decent, and pretty properly dressed young woman. He placed her age between twenty-two and twenty-five. As was his manner when he received an unexpected guest, he stood beside his desk and folded his arms across his chest.

"Please have your seat," he mumbled before she could speak.

"Thank you, sir. My name is Alaba."

"Okay. How can I help you?"

She clasped her hands on her laps. "We need your help, sir. The police came and took Amanda away." She blinked, worry etched around her forehead.

She had big, beautiful eyes, and knew how to use them to catch a man's attention. CJ, for a second, wondered if these girls were just human wraps of seduction or what?

"She sent you to me?"

"No. But I remember Nikky gave me your phone number some time back, when my boyfriend needed advice."

CJ could not remember her boyfriend, even if she gave a name. Many people came to him for "advice" all the time and if he decided to lump these together, he'd have made millions from just that. But first, Amanda.

He frowned. "What did she do?"

Alaba dragged in a deep breath. "I don't know. They just came and she tried to resist but they took her away."

He mentally rolled his eyes, his heart already thudding at the mere fact that he would see her again. Friday night was the worst time to get picked up because no one would bail her until Monday morning. He groaned. He had that brief to complete and present!

"Do you know where she is?"

"I ran after them, begging and asking where they were taking her. It's the station close to our house."

The one where he'd filed a complaint about Nikky and not gotten any response. No surprises there. CJ wanted to leave immediately but it would be madness and professional idiocy. He checked his watch. He couldn't be in that area of town for another one hour anyway. 8 pm was way too late to do anything unless he called on a "friend" in the police force.

He glanced at Alaba and saw how anxious she seemed. Her fingers twisted in between themselves and those huge eyes could swallow him up.

"I can't leave now, believe me."

"Please, she—"

"But I will be there tonight. When I finish up here."

Her head dropped and her shoulders slouched. "Well, thank you."

He wasn't fazed. "You're welcome." She headed for the door and he stopped her. "Alaba!"

She turned. "Sir?"

"You don't have to worry. I'll take care of it."

She curtseyed. "Thank you, sir."

"Hmm, surprisingly decent," he murmured after she was gone, before his heart resumed its anticipatory thump.

The last time he saw Amanda, he had thought would be the last. She was rude, had asked him to leave, threatened to "wound" him, whatever that meant. Besides, she had been indecently dressed, wet from a recent bath, and tempting as hell. He'd gotten a cold shower when he got home, hoping to cool off and it hadn't helped. However, he couldn't bear to indulge in thoughts about Amanda at the moment. She was not in any known danger and he was willing to pull a string on her behalf, though she didn't deserve it.

He called his friend at police headquarters. One of the best parts of being a lawyer was having easy access to policemen. The men in uniform were by far the neediest of legal bailouts.

"DSP, good evening,"

The man sounded as though distracted and paused after every word. "Barrister. Hello. Ah. How are. You."

"Did I get you at a bad time?"

"My brother. It's. It's. Weekend."

CJ sighed. "Let me call you back."

A rustling sound took over the background and CJ held his phone away from his ear. It lasted only a couple of seconds.

"Sorry about that, Barrister. Ehen, what were you saying?"

"I need your help. Tonight, sir."

When CJ hung up, he wondered if he should have contacted a much lower officer. He had them in numbers at his fingertips.

9

—·—

The moment CJ walked into the police station, three hours later, he was glad he'd called a deputy superintendent of police and not just a sergeant. Amanda was behind the counter, but she had been beaten up. Her face was swollen and her lip split. To CJ's surprise, the DSP had come over himself and taken her out of the cell, and all they waited for was to have her released to her "lawyer."

He was given a form to fill and sign, and then he took her, with anger and gratitude whirling through him. If she had been left in this place until Monday, she'd have been killed. It was unusual for a detained criminal to be beaten in the cell. Though it happened when the detainee was involved in a cult or some other group activities. Especially as a woman. She would have to tell him the whole story behind this.

She spoke for the first time after they were inside his car. "Thank you."

"You're welcome," he mumbled. "I'll pick you up tomorrow morning. Rest tonight and we can discuss tomorrow."

"I don't want to go to my house."

He stole a glance at her. "Why? And where do you want to go?"

She shrugged. "I don't know. Who told you to—Alaba?"

"Yes. She was genuinely concerned."

She rested her head back and closed her eyes. "Please, take me to my church."

"Church. I thought you don't have a church." He smirked. "Do they have a bathroom and a bed there? You need a good bath and good food. Sleep, rest."

"I don't have anywhere else."

She looked like she would sleep off at any moment. "Where's your church?"

She mumbled the address. It wasn't far, and he drove there. No way was he taking her to his house, if that was her intention. The building wasn't a big one and sandwiched between two houses. Amanda got out of his car and walked slowly to the entrance. He waited to see what would happen, his mind reeling and considering. Was it safe to leave her here? After about a minute, a man opened the door. She didn't even look back as she stepped inside. He took several calming breaths and convinced himself he owed her nothing, then sped off.

Still, he was restless and couldn't wait for morning to break. When he got to the church early the following morning, the man who had let her in opened for him. He was a security man, and this made him a little relaxed. As he had thought, there was no bathroom in the church so he decided to take her somewhere to clean up and then they could talk.

"It's a small place I manage for my friend. They're walk-in apartments, fully furnished, and one is unoccupied." He pulled into the Saturday-morning forming-traffic. "I just need to get to my house to pick the keys."

"Okay. Thank you."

She stayed in the car while he went inside to get the keys. She needed a change of clothes too, and reluctantly, he picked two of Nikky's outfits. He took some toiletries as well, and a spare towel.

"I'll just stop at a 24-hour filling station and get some snacks," he said as he got back into his car.

The ride to Yemi's block of ready-to-use flats on Opebi was a quiet one. CJ appreciated it because he had too many questions to ask her and didn't want to lose his temper while driving as he realised, he was prone to doing when with her. She seemed withdrawn, humbled but who wouldn't be? If he had not intervened, she'd be in police custody all through the weekend.

CJ opened the door to the only empty unit of the four available. The idea to have short leases of nothing more than three months on these units had paid off more than he or Yemi imagined. They kept the apartments well-maintained and so even when not occupied, they were clean, aired, and ready-to-use.

He placed the supplies on the island in the open kitchen area, built a lot like foreign homes with the small living area attached.

"There are two bedrooms and two baths. You can use any of them." He reached out to her with the small bag he packed. "When you feel ready to talk, come back out here."

She collected it. "Thank you."

He stared after her as she walked toward one of the doors that led to the bedrooms. She had a beautiful figure, he had to admit, the perfect hourglass, and her backside was incredibly heavy for her slim waist. CJ shook his head and turned away. He couldn't think of her in any way other than what she was, a stranger. Trouble.

Moments later he heard the shower and took out his laptop to avoid thinking of what was going on inside the house. He had always had a lot of work to do. Being a criminal lawyer got him a lot of good deals. Many times, his learned colleagues had asked how he could get the worst enemies-of-the-public off the hook, and he asked them how they could look a mosquito in the eye. Same way, he'd say. He never saw a criminal as one, but a person who needed to fight for a right to be free to do what they pleased. He had a conscience, he was helping people, and the money was pretty good.

A good one hour later, the sound from the shower went off and he gasped at how long she had indulged but he would too after the kind of ordeal she must have gone through. He closed his laptop in anticipation of his meeting with her, but after several minutes, running to another hour, he walked over to the door and knocked. When she didn't respond, he opened the door slowly and found her sprawled on the unmade mattress, fast asleep. Despite himself, he smiled and closed the door. She needed it.

10

— · —

Amanda had her fair share of men and what they could do with her. She wasn't only brain-wise, she was street-smart. If she warned anyone, she would hurt them, it was only because she could. She wasn't one to mince her words, especially when it came to protecting herself, because ever since she was a child, she had fought her own battles. But CJ didn't know that. And she wanted things to remain the way they were between them. She would never have sent for him, but rather sort herself out. She knew how to get out of difficult situations. Of course, to have a DSP come to her rescue at his call, left nothing to comprehend how important he was. At that time of the night? People hardly impressed her, but CJ did. She could confess to herself she found him extremely attractive, and that was admitting a lot because she didn't like men, only used and dumped them. And this was the more reason why she had to get him out of her business as fast as possible. She hated to have any type of weakness for anyone. She'd end up doing whatever they wanted and that was a type of vulnerability she couldn't afford.

So, when CJ knocked on the door a few minutes after she rested her head on the pillow, she closed her eyes and breathed easy, as she had done on numerous occasions for numerous men. It worked and he left her alone. For one, she needed to take the time to compose herself, but more importantly, she had to set the pace of their interaction. She would go to talk to him, at her own time, when she was ready, and not when he wanted.

The dreaded talk did not happen until three hours later, and two more checks from CJ. She wore her dirty spring dress because she didn't want to touch Nikky's clothes he packed for her. Hers was not dirty anyway, just rumpled a lot, and stained where she bruised. She had washed patches of it with the nice soap he added in the bag.

She walked into the parlour, her face diverted from his general form, and found a single seat. From her blindsight, she could see him follow her with his gaze. He waited for several seconds before he closed his laptop.

"What happened to you?"

She yawned. "When?"

"Listen, I don't plan to spend all day babysitting you. Are you going to talk or not?"

For the first time, she raised her eyes and looked at him. "Do I have a choice?"

"Definitely."

"I don't want to talk."

She couldn't believe she was saying this. She needed his help. A man who could get a DSP to come at that time of the night to free her was definitely what she needed. But pride and fear held her bound. It was the same reason she didn't stand up the two other times he checked on her. Though she'd been able to catch some sleep, she was a feather-light sleeper and each time he opened the door, she became aware.

He held her gaze until she looked away. To her surprise, he stood but didn't leave. Instead, he walked to the island.

"The food is cold, but we can put it in the microwave. You must be hungry."

The last thing she wanted was his pity. "I don't want to eat, and you can leave. I'll find my way to my house." She threw her head back on the chair and stared at the suspended ceiling. "Thank you for everything."

She heard him put the food in the microwave and start it. His every movement registered in her brain as he opened the fridge and took the drinks out.

"Your waist is too thin. You should eat."

She closed her eyes to ignore his comment. When the heating was done, he brought out the food to her.

"You must eat. And you must talk."

She did not acknowledge him. Instead, she breathed softly as though she was sleeping off. He nudged her slippered feet.

"Come on," he mumbled.

"What do you want?"

"Eat and talk."

She took the plate of hot fried rice and chicken, and it wasn't until it touched her mouth, she realized how very hungry she was. After the first several spoons, she slowed down, knowing he assessed her. At this point, she needed to be in total control of her senses.

"Why I was beaten by some boys from campus? I don't know. Apparently, they wanted Nikky and feel I know where she is."

She took another two spoons and when she finished munching, spoke. "Why I was arrested, the same reason. Same people."

He did not say anything until she finished eating and kept her plate aside.

"Can you give me the names of the boys?"

She snickered. "I don't have a death wish."

He leaned against the island. "I will provide protection for you."

"Why? You don't owe me. The opposite, in fact."

CJ narrowed his eyes. "I don't know why. Maybe I just want to be on top of issues with you. I don't like being interrupted at work to go on a rescue mission."

She leaped to her feet. "And I sincerely apologize. Alaba panicked. With Nikky missing, and I being taken, she must have felt she'd be next."

CJ laughed. "So, you don't think Alaba was concerned about you?"

She walked to the door. "It's the way of things and I don't hold it against her."

"What's the way of things?"

She gripped the doorknob. "Look, you were very kind to get me out of the cell. But the people who put me there are not going to disappear. Thank you very much, and don't worry yourself about me."

He walked slowly over, and she would have opened the door and left if he was someone else. But she owed him, the least being "not rude." When he should have stopped to respect her space, he continued moving closer until his lips touched hers. She turned her face away. It was just too much, the electric-currents between them. He held her chin and turned her back to him, and she pushed him. Whatever impression he might have of her was wrong, and she had no contest making it clear.

She opened the door, but he kicked it shut with his foot.

CJ breathed. "I'm not done here."

"Listen to me, I don't need you, okay?" But her breathing was hitched, and much as she tried to sound normal, she couldn't. "If there's anything more you want, let me know." She braced to catch his gaze. "If you try to touch me again, I'll hurt you in a way you'll never forget."

He smiled. "I'm not afraid of you."

"Then let me go."

"Where are you going? Back to your house for the boys to return?"

She held his gaze, despite herself. "I take care of myself."

"It shows." He leaned against the door. "Go and sit down and let us talk about your future."

For a long moment, she struggled with it. She hated interference, and from someone she already felt so vulnerable wasn't a good thing by a long shot. Still, her feet made up her mind for her and she walked back to her seat and took it. He drew in a long, ragged breath and followed her. After another extended period of silence, while she knew they were both trying to figure out where to draw the line, he spoke.

"What's your next plan?"

She had this well-thought out. "I have my final exams this coming week so I'm going to find a way to lay low until I finish, then I'll return to my house and face whatever."

"What course are you studying?"

"Law."

11

—　·　—

"**L**aw!"

CJ hadn't expected she was in his profession. Not as though there was any way to know.

"Yes, what did you think?"

He shrugged. "I don't know. You didn't say. I'd have expected you to at least mention it."

"When?" She rolled her eyes. "We haven't had a down-time, have we? To relax and gist."

"Your sarcasm does nothing for the situation you're in."

"Please, I need to go now, if there's nothing more to say or do."

He accepted they were not getting anywhere. But this was only because she refused to talk to him. He knew he had to find a way to get the truth out of her. She seemed truly tired and anxious to leave but to where? Despite that he'd made it clear he didn't want anyone coming to him unexpectedly, he wanted to help. He didn't understand where that came from, but it was there. He was attracted to her physically, which spoke tons about his decency, non-existent, and the way she rejected him hurt more than she realized. He felt ashamed of himself, and ideally, he should just let her go but he couldn't.

"Let me make this clear. I'm not allowing you to leave until my questions are answered."

She straightened. "Then ask them."

"Who are the boys?"

"I know only one of them. He's supposed to be a friend, our friend, Nikky and me." She sighed. "He's been looking for Nikky."

"For what?"

"I don't know. And that is heaven's truth."

He liked to pace when he asked important questions. Right now, he'd have to piece her answers together to form a story. He felt like a glass of brandy.

"Sure. So Nikky owes them and they believe you know where she is."

"Yes."

"Where's Nikky?"

She rolled her eyes again. "If I knew, I won't be here."

"When are you finishing your exams?"

"I have a paper every day of this coming week, then I'm done."

He clasped his hands. "I'm going to make an offer." He stared at her, but her gaze was averted. "I'll let you stay here for a week while you write your final papers. And then—"

She stood. "Thanks, but no thanks."

"Why? You need help."

"Why? Why would you want to be a part of my mess?"

CJ shrugged. "Because you called me into it."

"I didn't call you this time, Alaba did. And she's trying to save her own neck, believe me."

"Well, I'm interested in helping you or her, whichever." He took a step closer to her. "I don't feel comfortable Nikky is still missing and if there's a chain reaction to that, I am interested."

She smirked. "So interested you tried to kiss me just now."

She had to rub it in, but he owned it. "Yes. So interested I tried to kiss you." He threw up his hands. "I lack good morals. Thank you. Can we move on to a solution now? I'm not backing out of your mess, get that!"

She heaved a heavy sigh. "You want me to stay here for the week of my exam?"

"Yes. Do you have better ideas?"

"Staying here doesn't keep the boys away. They know where to find me in school. They are students." She sighed. "And this place is so far from school."

"You can Uber." He pulled out his credit card. "And as for your security in school, I'll get you an escort."

She gasped and then laughed. "Please give me a break. First, I don't need your money, and I don't want an escort. What kind of escort?" She slumped back into her seat. "Oh, I'm finally finished!"

He took his phone and dialled. "Major Ahmad! It's your boy, CJ." He laughed. Amanda sat forward and glared at him and he returned her gaze. "Yes, sir. Yeah." He paused. "I'm in a terrible mess. My small sister is being harassed by cult boys on campus." He listened then laughed. "No, sir. No. I just need one of your boys to follow her to campus for this week. While she writes her final exams." She covered her face. He hid a smile. "Yes, she's studying law too, final year." CJ laughed. "Yes, sir! I'm always at your service." He nodded. "Thank you so much, sir. I'll pick him up on Monday morning. Yes. Before six! Yes, sir. Thank you." He hung up. "Done."

She dropped her hands and stared at him. "What?"

"You have a soldier to escort you from Monday to Friday."

"Thank you."

"Good." He clapped. "I'll pick him up and take him to Faculty of Law. He will be in uniform and with a gun. He'll be waiting for you when you arrive. I'll tell you exactly where to meet him and what his name is."

"Hmm, thank you." She pressed her lips together. "And what do I owe for all of this?"

"Nothing. For now. I want to find Nikky too. She was my fiancée."

She stood, and then sat. "I guess I'm stuck here until my exams are over, and then I can have a life again."

"Yes. Precisely."

"I need to well, you don't have to worry about that."

He arched his eyebrows. "What?"

"Nothing. I'll–I'll be fine."

She was lying again. There was that little tilt of her lips when she did, and he didn't even think she was conscious of it. But he let it pass. He would not offer her money or any other thing. He had gone far enough with her and she'd made it clear she was a big girl.

"Okay then. You have my number if you need me. Call." He carried his laptop and stowed it away into its bag. "If you need anything—"

"I'll be fine. Thank you."

He wanted to ask if she would want to go to church the following day or would need to pick her clothes and books. But he controlled the urges. He knew he would not rest until this week was over but in his heart of hearts, maybe after her exams she'd leave the city or go and stay with her family and be out of his radar, and he could breathe again.

Amanda did not stand or see him off. At the door, he turned and gave her one last look. She averted her gaze, and he left, a hollow in his heart.

On the way back to his house, he called Yemi. It was getting to dusk.

"Guy, how are you?" he said. "I need you to please check up another number for me, please."

"Not on your life, CJ."

"Please. Are you at work?"

Yemi grunted. "For another three hours at least."

He called out Amanda's number, which he had subconsciously memorized. "Look, this is important. She is Nikky's roommate. There's a suspicion she's linked to Nikky's disappearance."

Yemi laughed. "You are still on this Nikky's matter? I told you the girl has changed her number and moved on."

"The question is why would she do that? She'll be writing her final exams this month. Why will she bail and run?"

"Who told you she bailed and ran. She's there on campus, living the life. Laughing at you from a distance."

"Her roommate doesn't know where she is."

CJ could almost see Yemi's shrug. "So?"

"So, she's missing. Please Yemi, track the number for the past one month. Please." "He called it out again.

"Why?" Yemi sneered. "You want me to lose my job?"

"We will sue your company, if you do. I help criminals but my second specialization is employment and labour."

Yemi laughed. "It's true what they say about criminal lawyers. You're as criminal as the guys you defend."

CJ rolled his eyes. "Thank you."

Yemi emailed the breakdown for Amanda's calls and text messages later in the evening with the message, "Print and delete email."

Her records were as clean and boring as a nun's. CJ couldn't help but think she must have another number she didn't give him.

12

— · —

The exam officer would not have allowed a uniformed soldier, an orderly, wielding his rifle inside the examination hall, but this guy had a permit. He refused to disclose who he was protecting either. After Amanda met him at the designated place, he'd told her to act normally, which was exactly what she wished.

With an empty house all to herself, she had left soon after CJ and returned to pack her clothes and books. She got her ATM card as well. Thankfully, Alaba had a guest so she'd been able to escape with just a flimsy explanation, but with a promise to say more later.

She bought some snacks at a supermarket nearby and Uber-ed back to the apartment in Opebi. She had to study because she could not afford to fail a single course. With the way her grade-point had plummeted over the years, she couldn't even afford anything less than a "C" if she planned to graduate. She made the bed, stocked her snacks, folded her clothes into the walk-in wardrobe, and slept for four hours. When she woke up after midnight, she studied until the early hours of the morning. Then slept a little more and went to church.

Monday went without incident but on Tuesday morning, the boy nick-named Slopo was waiting for her at the entrance of her exam hall.

He pressed her side against the wall at a corner, and whispered in her ear, "You used bottom-power to bail? Ehn, Amanda?"

She whispered back. "Let go or you'll get hurt."

Slopo laughed. "Talking tough? Come with me, let me teach you a lesson."

But neither got to move. The orderly closed up on them and hit Slopo with the butt of his gun. The boy slumped. Amanda hurried away as though she wasn't involved in any way. Because this was a public place, she didn't wait to see who saw what happened, but slipped into the hall and took a seat right in front in the middle. Once she was done with her exam, she called for an Uber.

Alaba found her at the side of the road. "Amanda! *Na wa* for you o, where have you been?"

Amanda glanced at her. "Hiding and writing my exams. Where else?"

"You just disappeared. Do you know how many people have come to look for you and Nikky? Will you tell me what's going on?"

The Uber arrived. "I have to go, Alaba. You know why I can't see anyone!"

"You girls should not get me into trouble o! Even me, I'm leaving that house." Alaba screeched. "I'm leaving."

Amanda got into the car and the driver moved. She rested her head on the back of the seat and stifled a sob. She had to go in search of Nikky as soon as she was done with school or she could turn up dead, especially when they all got to know what happened to their ringleader today. The orderly had been professional, and this made her feel safe but then what afterward? She would be back to her unprotected, volatile life.

She would not, could not trust CJ who Nikky had sang about barely a month ago. She'd have thought he would miss her so much; he'd go after her especially with all the people he had boasted of knowing. One minute he seemed concerned and the next, he was ogling her, his fiancée's supposed best friend. Of course, there was no way she could let him in on her life or her true relationship with Nikky. The earlier she disappeared from his vicinity, the better for her.

She'd found a church close to the house she stayed in and this was where she used as her address when getting an Uber. She felt safer entering a public place. Besides, she wanted to worship. Her new-found faith was the only hope she clung to. She had carried too much garbage for too long, she couldn't but hold on to God now.

The driver drove off and she walked into the church premises. The hall was open, and she found a seat at the front. It helped to be sure she hadn't been followed by some chance, and she seized the opportunity to pray. When she was done, she walked the five minutes it took to her new accommodation and let herself in. She only breathed after she had secured the lock.

****

Torts! The most dreaded of her papers was the last. Amanda wrote with all her being. She must pass this course as with the others. She'd spent all night studying, battling the dreaded events that would follow after she was done, and praying to concentrate.

None of the boys had come near her after the event with Slopo but she knew they were watching and waiting. And even with the promise of the orderly to see her into her taxi as he'd done every day of the week, Amanda looked behind her shoulder all the way to the road. She saw nothing and no one to suspect but it didn't mean they were not waiting. She dropped at the church and stayed indoor for almost four hours before she felt safe enough to venture out. Even then, she had her change of clothes, with a scarf to disguise, and she waited until a church service closed. These people knew her inside-out. They had her exam schedule, knew when she'd be done. She couldn't risk anything.

Her heartbeat was on a double when she got to her accommodation. She had her stuff packed. Since Saturday when he left, CJ hadn't called or checked on her, except on Monday when he gave her the details of the orderly, and he had been straight-to-the-point. If he had expected her to contact him, then, he didn't know her. He was the next person she needed to avoid. All he wanted was sex, and if she had anything to do with that, he'd never have it. She didn't like the way she reacted around him either so for two good reasons, she needed to be far from him.

To find Nikky. Nikky wasn't safe. Her friend could be anything, but an absconder wasn't one. And in all fairness, she had wanted to write her final exams as well. To marry CJ!

Despite all the stupid flings, Nikky had hoped to marry the rich lawyer.

She slammed the door behind her a little too loud and jumped when a voice behind her spoke as she turned the locks.

"Don't bother. I'm here already."

13

Amanda didn't tell him when she'd be done with her exams, but he'd gotten her timetable, and gone the extra mile to memorize it. Her last paper was at one and would last for three hours. CJ figured she'd get an Uber and rush from school as she'd done every day of the week. The orderly had reported the incidence on Tuesday morning, but all had gone smoothly since then. It only gave him the reason to believe she wasn't safe, and he needed to continue to protect her whether she liked it or not.

Somehow, it miffed him that he missed her. She occupied his thoughts day and night and he couldn't wait for Friday to be here. He had no intention of disgracing himself as he'd done previously when she rejected his advance. He suspected she was playing hard to get but for a girl like her, it was only a matter of time. Girls like her, and Alaba, and Nikky...campus girls! They all had a price tag on their heads. Name the right price and they'd do anything! He wondered how Nikky could have deceived him into thinking he could marry her. Such a slut! Yet, he closed from work after lunch and drove to Opebi to wait for Amanda.

He had a master key to the house and hoped to finish his work before she returned.

The fenced compound had a tall gate and a security post manned by a security company CJ paid to guard the property day and night. There was enough parking at the front too, and the guard opened the gate for him. He came out of his car a moment before he saw a young man walk to the door of Amanda's accommodation. He opened it with a key and went in. CJ stood for a long moment and glared at the door, unsure of what to do.

She already had a man come to stay with her? He thought angrily.

The security man called out. "Welcome, sir."

CJ summoned to him and he hurried over. "Who entered Flat 1 just now?"

The young man turned to the direction of the door as if to confirm the question. "Huh, the aunty living there. Her friend."

"Her friend? He...when did he start coming? She just came here for a short time."

"Yes, sir. He came Wednesday and left. Yesterday, he entered and left before she return. But I close so I didn't see her to tell her." The guard looked at the door warily. "Is there a problem, sir?"

"No, go back to work."

"Yes, sir." He bowed and returned to the security post, stealing one more glance at the door.

CJ got back into his car and drove around to the back of the one-story building. When he advised Yemi to buy the house, he had people who wanted to relax and enjoy themselves in mind, and though they hadn't gotten to getting a swimming pool yet, there was adequate space at the back for one. He parked the car on the side of Flat 2 and walked to the one he was after. First, he peeped into the bedroom Amanda had used, and saw two young men asleep on the bed. He could hear the humming of the air-conditioner. It took him a moment to gather his emotions.

There were three boys in the parlour, and they talked easily. All were dressed in black T-shirts and jeans. No, CJ didn't think Amanda knew about this, and even if she did, he was going to burst the party. Did the security man know there were so many boys in the house? CJ returned to his car and pulled out his pistol from under his car seat. He wasn't a "joking" criminal lawyer, and he was licensed to carry a gun. He had at least three hours to waste before Amanda returned. He took his laptop and went into the space created for a shower room for the "proposed" swimming pool, and though it was the most uncomfortable position, he sat on a slab and worked on an opening statement in a new criminal case. He had a good view of the gate from there.

When it got too dark, and the security lights went on with Amanda nowhere in sight, he moved on to his second plan and let himself into the flat through a fire escape exit no one used. He sat in the small passage and listened to the voices in the house; the boys smoked weed and cracked stupid jokes.

****

Amanda would never scream even if her life depended on it. She glared at the five campus boys waiting for her inside.

"It took you a long time oh, where did you go?" Slopo said.

She breathed hard. "Church."

All the boys laughed. Only Slopo spoke.

"Ah, that's true. You said you're now an SU." He snickered. "I should come and believe you, *abi*. When my head is still correct." He stood. "Where's the video?"

"I told you I don't have it. Nikky does."

"You want to die? Where's Nikky?"

"Slopo!" Amanda shrugged. "I don't know."

He was close enough and he slapped her hard.

"You don't like yourself!" A gun clicked, and a shot rang. "On your knees, all of you!"

Amanda gasped as CJ walked in slowly, his gun pointed at Slopo who had just been shot in the leg and was rolling in a fast pooling blood, crying. The other boys fell on their knees. She slid beside Slopo and went to stand behind CJ, effectively putting him between her and the boys.

"Lie face down or I will blow all your brains out," CJ shouted. Without turning away from the boys who quickly obeyed, he said, "Call the attention of the security man. He knows what to do."

"Yes, sir."

Amanda hurried to do CJ's bidding. She was still so shocked to find Slopo and his boys in the house. It meant she was right. They had trailed her, found where she was and laid in wait for her to be done with her exams. Maybe they assumed the soldier watched over her here too, and when they realized he didn't, came.

The security man at the gate called for the police and within the twinkling of an eye, a truck full of uniformed men arrived and took the boys away. The officer-in-charge, a fair-skinned, slender man took pictures of the scene himself, and afterward, invited CJ and Amanda to the station to give statements. It was going to be a long night, and much as Amanda was glad CJ had come to her rescue, she just couldn't help but wonder if it would not have been better to fall into the hands of Slopo and his boys. They would beat her again but would leave her to be harassed another day. The police, on the other hand, had too many issues. Since she wasn't the focus of attention this time, she hoped she could be back in time to deal with CJ. She had many questions for him and wanted to be rid of him so she could move on to the next things in her life. She could only hope.

CJ had to identify himself and produce the license for the gun, especially because government had just revoked gun licenses for citizens. They were both questioned for several hours and in the end, CJ called a lawyer from his firm to come over and "bail" them out even though they were not detained. Amanda wondered why he didn't call his DSP friend again but thought it might be too much too soon.

He didn't say a word all the way back to the apartment. Slopo's blood smeared the floor, and Amanda mentally thanked God it wasn't rugged. She could clean it up with the detergent she bought earlier. Overall, there was no permanent damage except the boys had smoked and dirtied everywhere. CJ dropped into the couch and closed his eyes while she did all of the cleaning. What could she tell him to get herself away from this mess she was in? Basically, what lie would he believe that would allow her to pack and disappear. He had gone into great lengths to help her, but she just wanted to be left alone now.

When she was done, she carried her duffel bag and entered the sitting room. To her surprise, he was fast asleep. She could slip away. Here and now. It was past midnight and she doubted she would get an Uber or a taxi, but that wasn't a problem. She would find a church, there were many on the street and being Friday, a few may be having night vigils. Once it was morning, she'd start on her way and send him a message to thank him. It was brilliant.

She tiptoed to the door and opened it. One quick look at the sleeping-CJ, she opened and shut the door as quietly as she could. The new security man on duty greeted her casually. She exited and faced the direction of her church, walking as fast as she could. She was right, a programme was going on inside. She entered, smiled at the usher at the door, and found two seats at the back in the corner. She hurried to take one, happy she could easily sneak out when she needed to. She'd hardly drawn in a sigh of relief when someone occupied the seat next to her.

"Amanda, or what do you call yourself?" CJ whispered. "What manner of clown are you?"

14

Fortunately, the prayer session started. CJ whispered in her ear that he had his gun.

Amanda whispered back fiercely. "You dare not use it inside the church."

He stifled a chuckle. "Don't dare me. We are going back to the house. Now."

"No."

He held her elbow and lifted her quite easily. "I'll carry you if you don't cooperate."

She did, even smiled at the usher at the door. He led her to his car, had her sit in the back, and it wasn't until he had the child-lock secured did he tell her they were going to his house.

"For your information, the DSP who helped to free you sent me a message. Apparently, young woman, you are indeed a criminal wanted for many crimes," he said.

"So, take me back to the police station and wash your hands off me."

He snorted. "Why are you so eager to get rid of me?"

"Because you are no longer useful to me."

"You are a wanted criminal. I am a lawyer." He stole a glance at her in the back-view mirror, but she just stared ahead. "When we get to my house, you will tell me why you are wanted. And what happened to my fiancée."

The words were meant to trigger a response. He got none. The roads were free at that time of the night, so they got home on time, but he had no intention of going to sleep. She had to open up to him this time and he wasn't taking any other thing from her.

He opened his refrigerator and removed bread and butter. "I'm hungry. It's been a hell of a night."

She walked over to his couch and seemingly changed her mind and took a single chair. It didn't matter to him. He didn't offer her any food either. He got a bottle of Coca-Cola and took the couch she had despised.

"Talk," he said around the bread in his mouth. When she didn't respond, he continued. "Where did you go when you finished your exam?"

Amanda exhaled. "The church. I was afraid they will follow me."

"They followed you. Why?"

"Listen, I carry a lot of dung with my life. And I don't want you involved."

"I'm a big boy. I'm not afraid of you. And I am involved already." He opened his phone and handed it to her.

She took it and read the message from DSP asking him to turn her over or he'd be "aiding and abetting" a criminal.

"What did you do?"

She held the phone with her two hands for several seconds. "This is your chance to turn me in and forget about me. I'm not worth it."

He stared at her bowed head, slouched shoulders and defeated demeanour. She was his "spec." The kind of people he worked for. Forget the fact that she was attractive as ever and he wanted to do more than was good at this time, he was interested in her case.

"Okay, you think you're not, but I think you are." He set his meal aside. "Listen to me, it's too late for both of us. I'm not backing down."

She slouched even further. "Nikky took a video during an...an operation and Slopo wants it. He thinks I have it."

"What operation?"

She frowned. "Drugs, robbery, prostitution. Slopo is an arranger. He gets girls, boys, anything. For money."

CJ felt his temperature rise. "You do all these too?"

"Before."

He arched his eyebrows. "Before what?"

"Two months ago." She stood and gave him her back. "They don't believe I have changed. That I don't want to be a part anymore."

"What made you change?"

"I found God." She cried. "I know it's difficult for anyone to believe. That's why I just wanted to finish my exam and leave."

"Leave to go where?"

She shrugged. "I had some money. I was thinking I'll just move to Aja or another part of town and get a job."

"Where's your family?"

She hugged her arms around her waist. "We…they are here in Lagos."

"Talk to me, Amanda." He went to stand close behind her. "I'm not leaving you, whether you like it or not. And if you think you're smart, I'm smarter. I've been dealing with criminals long before you started prostituting."

She cursed under her breath and he laughed. "Yes, babe. I'm closer to forty than thirty and I've been in this business longer than your twenty-five years."

She shifted away from him. "I'll only tell you because I want to. You're not as old as you say."

"Okay, I'm as old as I say but not done criminal law for as long as your age." He raised his index finger. "However, I have experience and don't ask me what."

"I'm not twenty-five."

"That's beside the point."

"Twenty-four."

"Close enough. Talk to me."

"My father threw my mum out when I was six. She had four of us." She shuddered. "Family got involved and begged him to take us back and he did. But things were never the same."

He didn't know how this answered his question but if she wanted to talk about it, then he'd indulge her. "How?"

"He had a new wife who he worshipped so we were dealt with by her and my father." She turned to face him. "I was on the streets before I turned seven."

"Did you get any venereal disease?"

His question had the expected result. She blurted the truth. "Of course not. Never."

"So, I'm safe," he muttered.

"I'm never going to have anything to do with you."

He arched his eyebrows again. "Then stop flaunting your body in my face."

Her mouth dropped open. "Please, can I leave now?"

"Where are you going?"

"Away."

He pointed at the seat she vacated. "Sit. And tell me about Nikky. Where is she?" He returned to his seat when she did hers.

"I don't know." She sighed. "But now I have to find her. With Slopo and all. And I feel responsible."

"Responsible? How?"

"Slopo didn't know about the video. The information slipped from me." She blinked. "So, I told Nikky to go away for a while, you know, give him space."

"What did she want the video for, anyway?"

Amanda shrugged. "To blackmail him. Everyone did it. I mean, you get better deals."

"Why didn't she just trade the video? Isn't that what you all do?"

Amanda rubbed the back of her neck. "Nikky asked for money, which is unusual. Slopo got angry with her."

"So where did Nikky leave to?"

Amanda covered her face. "I didn't mean to tell her about it. I panicked. There was a party in Abuja...I'm sorry."

CJ leaned forward. "Abuja?"

"She was supposed to be back Sunday evening. Slopo would have cooled down and Nikky would ask for something else. I was going to force Nikky to ask for something else. But she hasn't returned since." She dropped her hands and there were tears in her eyes. "You see why this is all my fault?"

It made no sense to him yet. She hid something and he planned to find out what.

"Do you have the video?"

Her gaze fell.

15

C J insisted they went to sleep. It was close to four in the morning and she didn't think she could sleep but he got her into his room, locked the door and pushed her on to the bed. Amanda could defend herself against any man. The only reason Slopo had gotten away was because there were more than two of them against her. All the years she spent hawking taught her street fight, and she would use the techniques she knew without restraint. But CJ didn't come near her. He entered his bathroom and when he returned, refreshed, he threw a blanket on the floor and slept. From her experience with him "sleeping" on the couch at the other house, she didn't bother with leaving, and she was very tired too. She closed her eyes and didn't wake up until CJ nudged her feet.

She sat up and looked around. The air-conditioning was really chilly, but she felt rested. CJ walked over to the window and peeped out.

"It's almost noon. DSP has called my number endlessly until I told him I don't know where you are." He glanced at her. "Get ready. We're going to Abuja."

While she gasped and tried to gather her thoughts, he walked out of the room.

His bathroom was a dream with a shower, and a Jacuzzi but Amanda could not indulge. She wore a pair of comfortable stretch jeans and T-shirt and joined him less than ten minutes later. He was on the phone with someone but arched his eyebrows when she walked into his sitting room. He pointed towards the dining table and she saw he had bought some food. Her stomach growled and she marched over, her duffel bag in her hand. She was travel-ready, and she still planned to disappear on him if she could. She didn't have many options, but she knew her way around.

He had been thoughtful enough to buy fried yam and egg sauce instead of the rice or snacks she'd been eating all week. The restaurant he got it from knew what good food tasted like and she gobbled it down. It was after she was filled that she noticed his outfit, black leather trousers with black fitted T-shirt and black snickers. Did he think they were going to war; she could almost laugh. He looked good though, and she mentally pinched herself for even having such a thought. They had both made it clear what the boundaries would be and any form of likeness for him had to be suppressed.

Amanda cleared the table, seeing he had eaten, and found the kitchen where she threw the disposable plates in the trash. If they were going to Abuja, she reckoned the dustbin would need to be taken out or it would stink. Like the rest of his house, the kitchen was big, and well-equipped, and surprisingly very clean. She guessed someone like him would have a cleaner or housekeeper, so she didn't bother about the trash anymore. She enjoyed cooking but with the kerosene stove she managed in her house, cooking had always been a pain. Alaba had better cooking equipment and Nikky never cooked but she had chosen to be frugal. She saved her money to pay for her education and the future. She could imagine herself owning such a space. The marble-top stretched to half of the wall and she slid her hand over it. She would try every type of recipes...

"Are you ready?"

She jumped and turned to fall right into CJ's arms. How did he walk up without making a sound?

"We need to talk about it," she said and moved aside.

He leaned against the sink. "Definitely. I have to know where I'm going in Abuja."

She took a deep breath. "Are we...I have to find out the place. I didn't have the full details."

"You're lying again."

She clasped her hands. "Not if I can help it. You are making everything more complicated." She moved further away. "If you really want to help me, allow me to go to Abuja alone."

He snickered. "You want to run away."

She gasped. "I have to."

"You don't trust me?"

She looked at her hands. "I can't trust anybody."

"Okay." He threw his hands up. "I'll let you go. Do you need money?"

She bit her lip. "No, thank you."

He waved toward the door. "Bye. Now, I can stop lying to the people looking for you."

She walked briskly to the sitting room and picked her bag. He didn't follow her, and she couldn't breathe until she got out and into a bus. From now, she couldn't afford an Uber. Every kobo needed to be saved and preserved. Her first port of call had to be Ronnie's room on campus. She had gone for the party too and set up the meeting with the girl she met in the Chemistry department. That girl wasn't going to help now. So, back to Ronnie. She wasn't lying about not knowing where to go in Abuja. Those parties took place in different places. The half-truth was that she knew who to contact to get the information. But she had to speak to the people who were there.

Ronnie, a tall, skinny girl in her late-twenties, and who had been a university student longer than anyone cared to know, was under a tree in the female hostel, smoking and joking around with two other girls. Amanda hurried over to her. She dragged on her cigarette and blew it into Amanda's face.

"You know they're looking for you?"

Amanda panted. "Slopo?"

The two other girls excused themselves and hurried off.

Ronnie shook her head. "Police. You don't know that video thing leaked."

"Ronnie, please I have to find Nikky. She—"

"Aha, but I told you to speak with that girl, I forgot her name. That one in Chemistry." She puffed.

"The girl was not helpful. She said she left Nikky there." Amanda frowned. "Please, *shey* you left on Saturday. Where was she?"

"You want me to give you the name of someone she spent the night with?" Ronnie spat, missing Amanda by a thread. "How will I know?"

"But you know the house. The—"

"Wo! I don't have the name or address of anything. Ask Slopo, or that boy that normally drives us from the park, I can't remember his name."

"Ronnie—"

The thin girl threw her cigarette on the ground and started walking away. "Look behind you, Amanda." Then she broke into a run.

From experience, Amanda knew she needed to run too, and not in the same direction as Ronnie. Without turning, she took to her heels in the direction of the female hostel, knowing it would be more difficult for whoever was behind to find her with so many girls and rooms to hide.

She barged into a room on the first floor and slid under a bed with shouts of, "Police! Hold it there!" behind her and more shouts and screaming from the girls. The door slammed shut and a girl poked her face at her.

"Please come out, we don't want trouble."

Amanda trembled. "Please, they will soon go."

"No o," another girl shouted from the top of one of five bunks in the crowded room. "We will call them for you o, or you quietly surrender yourself."

Amanda fumbled for her phone. "Please, please let me just call—"

The girl on the bunk shouted. "She's here. All these foolish girls."

Others shouted her down. One said, "Let her go on her own, *abeg*! I'm naked o! No police in here, please!"

Amanda fumbled with her phone and speed-dialled the first number on her list.

"Where are you?" CJ said in a breathy voice.

Someone banged on the door. "Police! We're coming in!"

The other girl shouted. "Abeg, I'm naked ooo!"

Footsteps hurried to the next door, the banging and police-shouting were repeated. Doors slammed. Amanda came out from under the bed and ran out of the room. It took a moment before she realized heavy footsteps chased after her. She could run, and these men wouldn't know this. She came back into open space and continued in the direction of the boys' hostel. Men didn't tell as much as women. She barged into a room and went under a bed. No one said anything and she wondered if there was anyone in the room. In the ensuing silence, she looked at her phone and saw CJ had hung up and sent a text. He wanted her location. She typed and sent it, and cuddled under the bed, now realizing it was smelly and musty. She closed her eyes, dreading what she lay on and the stink she'd need to get off her body afterward.

16

CJ arrived in the room an hour later. He knocked on the door she told him she "suspected" she entered and one of six young men lounging inside pointed to under a bed. Whatever those boys had under the bed needed sanitization. CJ nearly puked when he bent.

He stood quickly. "I'm here, babe."

Amanda crawled out and he turned his face from her. A few chuckles from around the room reminded him they had company.

"*Omo,* you need a bath." He exhaled. "I know where."

Instead of turning on the air-conditioning in the car, he wound down the windows and sped so enough air would come in. A five-star hotel, which he'd attended conferences at was just a few kilometres from the university and he drove there.

"I'll get you a room, and while you clean up, I'll wash my car." He sneezed. "Goodness, boys can stink."

He left her in the car to get the room and then returned to fetch her. She must have lain on rotten food and drink because her clothes were soaked through. She mumbled her gratitude before he left and he was only happy to be away from her, the first time for him to feel so. The hotel had a great carwash, so he drove to it and had his interior cleaned. Then he returned to the room.

Amanda had washed, from head to toe and changed into clean clothes. Her hair earlier tied in a bun was tied up in one of the hotel towels, and she smelt of perfumed soap and shampoo. She seemed subdued, which made him glad. He had thought she'd call on him but not so soon. It made him want to laugh. With the power on his side, he thought up several things he could ask or make her do, but he could see the stubborn way her lips were pressed together, and he didn't want to dare her to face any more risk.

He sat on the edge of the bed. "They caught one of the girls. Probably thought it was you."

"I'm sorry I called. I panicked."

He didn't plan to make things easy for her. "What do you want to do now?"

She covered her face for a second and then whispered, "What do you advise?"

It took all of his willpower to not laugh. He appreciated her inner will, though. At least she tried to set out on her own. She probably couldn't imagine how much of a mess she was in. He took his time responding. He didn't want her to know how much he'd like to walk away from her and all her troubles, yet stay and help, and get to know her better. The attraction he felt for her was just too profound to ignore.

"Well, the choice is yours at the end, you know." He sighed. "I want to help you, but you have to let me."

"Help me." She bowed her head. "Please."

CJ hid his smile. "When you left me and came here, what did you have in mind?"

She paced. "So, there was supposed to be a party and Nikky went for it. I came to ask one of the other girls, Ronnie, who went what happened to Nikky."

He arched his eyebrow. "You didn't ask earlier?"

"I had but this girl told me she left Abuja on Saturday and Nikky was supposed to leave on Sunday with the others." Amanda sighed. "She told me of another girl who stayed till Sunday, but the girl refused to disclose anything."

"So, why did you come back here?"

"To see Ronnie. I wanted the address of the party venue."

He knew what those parties were like. He had been a bad boy in university, done a lot of mischiefs, and had female friends who attended. It would likely be in a rich man's secret house. There would be a good supply of campus girls who would do anything the host and his friends wanted, basically disgusting orgies. The girls would be paid well and sent off at the end of the weekend. He tried not to visualize Amanda in one of those parties.

"Did she give you?"

"No. The police came after us before we could finish talking." Amanda moaned. "She told me the police were looking everywhere for me."

"They had your picture. I saw them leaving when I arrived."

"My picture?" Her eyes widened. "Who would have given them my picture?"

"I was surprised too." He stared at her. "Are there things you are not telling me? Because I know Slopo could not have from his hospital bed or police cell, wherever he is. Unless Alaba?"

She gushed. "Alaba?! Why would she give the police my picture?" Her voice grew tremulous, which indicated her desperation. "Honestly, I don't know what is going on. I know Slopo was after me and I've been feeling guilty about Nikky's disappearance, but I haven't done anything bad in a while."

The way she breathed hard had a strange effect on him and he turned away. He needed to subdue his basal feelings to coordinate his thoughts. The police had taken one girl away with them, and he didn't know why if they had truly come to look for Amanda. They also seemed to know exactly where to look. And he had confirmed DSP had nothing to do with this because the senior officer had only ranted that he didn't know she was such a criminal when he stepped in on her case.

"When I spoke with DSP this morning, he said the people who had you arrested are very angry he set you free. It's obviously not Slopo. Or is it? Do you know who got you arrested?"

He knew she was lying even before she spoke a word.

"No."

He stood. "Amanda, I'm leaving. Check out before noon tomorrow." He headed for the door.

"Nikky's mum."

He stopped but did not turn back. "Nikky's mum?"

She sobbed. "It's a long story, please understand, I didn't mean any harm. I was just so ignorant at the time. And angry."

CJ turned slowly. "Sit down. We have this room until tomorrow."

17

—·—

CJ was back on duty, in grill-mode as his colleagues called it when they saw him like this, but Amanda had no idea what he was about to subject her to. She sat as he indicated, her hands in her laps.

"Do you want a drink? Food?"

He checked his watch, it was close to seven and he doubted she'd had anything since the "yam and egg" breakfast. She shook her head.

"Let me order dinner, anyway." He walked to the phone box and placed a room-service order. "Let's have it in two hours' time, okay? Thank you." He hung up then sat on the stool by the dresser. "Start from anywhere, talk for as long as you wish. But I want to know everything."

She squared her shoulders. "Nikky met me when she got admission. I helped her with registration. Just because she was in my faculty, looking confused and new. So, I don't even know why because I normally mind my own business. She told her mother about me and the mum started joking I was Nikky's school-mother and she was handing her over to me." She twisted her fingers.

He got the message right there and if she didn't say anymore, he understood why Nikky's mother must be after her to find Nikky.

"How long ago was this?"

"Five years."

"How long have you been a student?"

"Six."

He nodded. "You couldn't have been her school-mother. You are close in age."

"Nikky was just fifteen."

"She told me she's twenty-six."

Amanda scoffed. "Nikky just turned twenty."

CJ arched his eyebrow. "In essence, you took her by the hand, and showed her the way."

She blinked away tears. "Yes," she whispered.

"I see." He smirked. "This is not even as long as I thought."

"At the time, I was just very angry and rebellious. I was paying for my own education because my father would not, and my mother refused to leave him." She flinched. "They really liked Nikky," she said softly. "The men...she was young and very beautiful." Tears slid from her eyes. "I was jealous."

"I think you're far more beautiful than Nikky." CJ mumbled. "That makes no difference to you, I guess."

She ignored his remark. "I gave her to them at every opportunity. To the worst of them. They smothered her with a lot of money." She looked up at him. "But she started to like it too."

CJ sniffed. He knew how much Nikky liked it. She was cheating on him with at least two other guys and flirting with another two. His fool-self had no clue. All five of them gave her a lot of money. He had given her a credit card in his name, and Nikky was the "queen of spending." He cringed at the thought that he had been having a relationship with a twenty-year-old girl. When she was fourteen, he was double her age!

"She lived with me. Her mother would not have her stay on campus or live with anyone else." She covered her face with trembling hands. "She would have been better off without me, and now she's missing." She sobbed.

And her mother is viciously after you.

He thought she'd continue speaking but she didn't and for a moment he wondered if she knew more. Quite alright, one should feel guilt for misleading a teenager and helping her choose a path to destruction, but Amanda's grief seemed to go deeper. So far, he didn't think she had told a lie. It was what she had not said that bothered him. In his profession, he knew a weeping witness was useless, so he decided to give her space. He took his laptop and opened a file for her. There was no way to avoid a case in this matter, with the police involved, she may end up in prison, but he had no plans on letting her know unless it became obvious.

"I suggest you rest. Tomorrow, we'll go to Abuja as planned and try and find Nikky."

She nodded and lay on the edge of the bed. He had Yemi's print-out of Nikky's phone records and he would use it to trace her movement if Amanda didn't have names and contacts. But he knew she did. There was no way she'd be so involved in all of that prostitution without knowing a few people here and there. He organized the case as he planned for it to move forward, making notes he'd present her to the police once they returned from Abuja. He made other calls to re-book the flight he cancelled and also booked a hotel for them. One double room, because he had no plans of having her out of his sight for one minute. She was prone to flight, and he was not deceived by her tears, even if he thought they were genuine.

****

Amanda closed her eyes and cuddled on her side, but she was not for once unaware of CJ in the room. He sat at the desk and punched away on his laptop. During her tales, he had not jotted a word, but she knew he paid rapt attention. Her heart thudded continuously. If she had known this would all end like this, she'd have not called him. The voice of her conscience blamed her but she argued she had not known he was such a person. A person who would not take "no" for an answer.

She had called Lanre, and Buddy, and Victor and Chief Hassan. They'd all told her Nikky knew how to take care of herself. Obinna had shown some concern but nothing more. Igwe promised to call back but didn't. All these guys' numbers she had found amongst Nikky's books when she searched. She knew Nikky's mother would hold her responsible, and she indeed felt so. She was the reason Nikky, an innocent fifteen-year-old church girl who had never even been kissed before, would become top-of-the-range campus whore...She couldn't forgive herself for "ignorantly" messing the other girl's life up, now she had become saved. It was her job to "save" Nikky and she had to do it or die trying.

For a long time, CJ continued to work, not paying her any attention until the food came. He opened the door and let the waiter in, mumbling where to keep the cart. Then he walked to her side and leaned over. She opened her eyes before he said anything.

"I sleep just as light as you. Maybe lighter," he said. "Food is here. I'm going to the lobby to take a call."

She sat up. "Okay." Her stomach rumbled and she wanted badly to eat.

He walked to the door. "Don't do anything stupid, you have a criminal case on your head."

She rolled her eyes all the way to the back after he left. The food beckoned and she opened the dishes to find jollof rice, fried plantain and roasted fish. Delighted, she dug in. There was only water in the refrigerator, and she drank from there and then remembered she needed to make a call. Nikky's brother, Akin.

He picked up at the first ring. "Where have you been? I thought you said you'd come after your exams!"

Amanda sighed. "I'm sorry. I went—"

"Where are you?"

"It's a long story. First, Slopo, the boy from school came. And then I wanted to get an address from—"

"We had an agreement, Amanda!" He barked. "All this one you're talking is story."

"The police came after me again." She cried. "You promised to keep them away until you see me."

"But you were nowhere to be found!" He paused. "And I didn't send any police after you. Mummy didn't either."

"Then who did? Everybody on campus said they came looking for me."

"Look, where are you?"

She told him the name of the hotel. "That lawyer Nikky was going out with said—"

"Come outside the hotel in thirty minutes. I'll come and pick you."

"Akin, please no police until I at least—"

"See you soon." He hung up.

She owed him. He was the reason she could sit for her exams without any harassment from his mother. And though she had made it clear they couldn't have a relationship, she respected and really liked him. Her mind whirled. It was best to follow him. She didn't know much about CJ, anyway. Though he had also helped her a lot, he'd made it clear he wanted to sleep with her, which made her uncomfortable. She could defend herself from any man, but he was also street-wise and had a gun he used without second thoughts.

Amanda covered her face and prayed to God to help her know what to do.

18

Yemi found CJ in the "smoking area" of the lobby, bent over his laptop. A bottle of Remy Martins brandy was already open on the stool beside him with his glass half-full and an empty glass. He looked up when his friend approached, and only waved him to the seat opposite without a word.

"What was so urgent at this time of the night, CJ?"

CJ raised his index finger, punched in some keys on the laptop and then gave his attention to Yemi. "Sorry, I wanted to be sure the contract doesn't have any error."

Yemi took the brandy and poured some into the empty glass. "Contract! That can't wait until morning or Monday! And why are you here?"

"I'm leaving for Abuja in the morning. I should have gone today."

Yemi took a sip. "What's happening in Abuja?"

"Work, unexpected. And I may be away for a couple days." He pushed the laptop to him. "Take a look. Read the clause especially."

Yemi drank all of the brandy in his glass as he read through. "This is good. Will they accept?"

"They can negotiate but they have to accept." CJ finished his drink and poured some more. "What's the least you can accept?"

Yemi shrugged. "I'll take a five-year-lease."

"A five-year-lease will not work. Nobody will take it. Ten years, at least."

"Hmm." Yemi arched his eyebrow. "There's nothing like seven-and-a-half?"

CJ smirked. "Do you see the amount? Are you okay with it?"

Yemi took a moment and scrolled through. "Wait a minute. Is this the farm?"

"Of course, what did you think? A castle in England?"

"Ah, ah, ah, wait a minute. I need to read it again."

CJ heaved a heavy sigh. "Take your time. You're the one who has a one-hour drive home tonight." He leaned back and sipped his brandy.

At some point, Yemi started to scan aloud, making a buzzing sound with his indistinct words but CJ ignored it as much as he found the sound irritating.

"The amount is not enough. Ten million for twenty years."

CJ shrugged. "You can only negotiate a lesser number of years to get more. It's barren land. To you, a bonus. Or something—" He stopped talking when he saw Amanda walking towards them with her bag slung over her shoulder.

She spared Yemi a glance. "Good evening. Sorry to interrupt."

Yemi whistled. "My father, my father."

CJ arched an eyebrow. "What is it?"

"I need to go. Someone...is here." She shifted her bag though he knew it wasn't heavy.

Yemi chuckled. "No wonder you are here, CJ, *omo-ita*."

CJ remained slouched though he could feel tension build up from his toes. "Who is...someone?"

"You have to give me her number, CJ. When you're done—"

"If you don't stop, Yemi, I'm calling Kemi now!" CJ snarled. "Yes?" He turned to Amanda.

Yemi threw up his hands. "Ah, *jor o*! The devil will not mess your life."

Amanda bit her lower lip. "Akin. Nikky's brother."

She blinked and he knew there was something. She could have sneaked away without his knowledge.

He stood. "Do you want me to come with you?" She nodded. He looked at Yemi. "Please give me a minute." Then back to Amanda. "Is he driving?"

"Uber."

Yemi followed them anyway. Outside the hotel lobby, they scouted the parking area but all the cars seemed parked.

"Call him that you're outside," CJ said.

Amanda did. "He's in a white Toyota Corolla at the end of the lot. He wants me to come over." She hung up.

CJ nodded. "Sure. Lead the way."

The Corolla was parked, and the driver and a man at the back, sat and waited.

Closer, CJ stepped forward. "Let me talk to him, first."

She nodded. With the parking lot so well-lit, it was easy to see the men in the car. CJ moved to the driver's side.

"He's in the back," she said but he leaned over to the driver instead.

"Hello, Detective."

"Ah, Barrister CJ," the driver startled.

Akin wound down his window and glared at Amanda. "You brought a lawyer."

She shook her head. "He's Nikky's boyfriend. I was trying to tell you on the phone that—"

"Who are all these people you came here with?" Akin squeezed his face. "Come on, enter let's go."

Yemi stepped up beside Amanda. "Where are you taking her to?"

CJ straightened. "He's here with a police officer, Amanda. Do you want to follow them?"

Amanda shook her head. She covered her mouth with her hand and CJ walked back to Akin's side where she and Yemi stood.

Akin shouted. "Amanda, you brought a lawyer, you think you're smart."

Amanda cried. "You said you will not bring police."

The police detective came out of the car and looked directly at Amanda. "Get inside."

CJ blocked her with his body. "Detective, talk to me."

"Barrister, she's a very bad girl, o. You should just hand her over to us."

"If you want me to bring her, I will but she's with me, let's respect ourselves."

Akin hit the inside of the car. "See this foolish girl, you think you can get away!" He yelled. "I will deal with you. You are very stupid. And you, lawyer! Were you not the last person to see my sister? Ehn?"

"Barrister, it's just because of you, o. Please bring her to our station. Tonight, if possible." The detective got into the car. "Mr. Akin, I know Barrister CJ very well. Let's go, he will bring her." He started the ignition.

"Go where?" Akin screamed. "Wait, don't move!"

The detective zoomed off. CJ followed the car with his gaze. "He wants to sleep with you, correct?"

"We were on and off," Amanda mumbled.

Yemi cackled. "Ah, not easy with a body like this, *ke*."

"Yemi!" CJ growled. "I'm calling your wife."

"*Jor*, leave that thing. Because you're not married? Where do you get them from, *sef*?" Yemi smiled at Amanda. "Will you give me your number?"

CJ pointed toward the entrance. "I still have work to do. And you have a one-hour drive back to your beautiful wife, mister!"

Amanda marched into the hotel, the men strolling in a more leisurely pace behind. CJ avoided staring at her retreating figure with her hips swaying so furiously in her hurry to leave.

Yemi stopped walking when Amanda disappeared into the elevator. "You think you want to involve yourself with her, though?"

CJ sighed. "I'm not only involved. I'm dyed-in-the-wool."

19

A friend of CJ, Joshua, picked them up at the airport. The men chatted unstopped through a fifty-minute drive to Joshua's house, while Amanda sat at the back of Joshua's jeep, reeling over what happened the night before. CJ had come up to the room close to dawn, reeking of alcohol, dropped into the couch and slept off in his day clothes. Their flight was at noon, and he'd woken up just in time for them to catch it. Someone at the airport had offered to drop his car in his house and pick them when they returned. The way he commanded people when he needed them continued to amaze her.

Joshua lived in Maitama, an upscale neighbourhood, and he took them there first. His wife, Mira, just had a set of twins and CJ wanted to see her. She offered them lunch but they both declined.

"Joshua will drop us off at our hotel, and then I have some work to do," CJ said with an apologetic tone.

"Hmm, Barrister CJ and work. Work is your life." Mira stole a glance at Amanda. "I still wait to meet that woman who will take you away from your files."

Joshua laughed. "She hasn't been born, my dear."

The hotel CJ booked was in Wuse 2 another classy area in Abuja, and he seemed to have a good relationship with the management as well. This time, they got a suite. CJ ordered a late lunch and after the meal, asked her to call her contact in Abuja.

Amanda called Eric, a pimp she'd known all her university days. He agreed to meet up at a *suya* garden not too far from their hotel. Eric wore a plain shirt and tie, over dark trousers and formal shoes. CJ arched an eyebrow when he approached their table. They could be colleagues. The men shook hands and CJ asked him to place his order.

"I can take smoked fish and beer," Eric said. "I have to be fast, Amanda. What's up?"

"When your order arrives, we can talk," CJ said.

Amanda glared at CJ with disapproval, but he ignored her, which annoyed her. But he seemed to know how to deal with people and she wasn't about to disagree with him in Eric's presence. They sat in silence until the waiter arrived with their orders. CJ had just water and she wanted nothing. Quietly she was glad CJ didn't drink any alcohol because that just could change everything if he got drunk again. She didn't know what kind of drinker he was, but he'd returned late and stoned the night before, and she had been glad he went to sleep on the couch immediately, and not come near her.

When the waiter left, Amanda swallowed. "Nikky didn't return to Lagos."

Eric leaned back. "Are we still talking about that? I told you I don't know why."

"But you saw her on Saturday and Sunday. When they were all leaving."

Eric shrugged. "So? They were all leaving."

Amanda heaved. "Didn't she say anything to you?"

"Like what?" He took a long swig of beer. "You know how things are when you people are leaving. Do you normally talk about your plans?"

CJ sat back, his fingers interlocked. "But she wasn't leaving. So, did she say anything to you?"

Eric paused in his downing. "Are you a policeman?"

CJ lowered his voice. "Just answer the question."

Eric took a big piece of fish and put in his mouth, preventing him from speaking. Amanda didn't know what else to make of it. Eric wasn't violent but he'd been a pimp probably all his life. He would sell his mother for a plate of food if he could. CJ dipped his hand in his jacket pocket and brought out a bundle of naira notes in different denominations. Eric swallowed quickly and took a gulp of beer.

"These girls will follow anyone with the money. They have no shame." Eric looked at Amanda as though he included her. Then actually said it. "You know yourselves."

Amanda could throw up at him. He was right though, but did he have to say it to her face?

CJ pushed the money to him. "Who did Nikky follow?"

Eric stuffed the bundle in his trouser pocket. "This boy, boasting he just came from Germany. Was waving dollars all over the place." He finished his beer.

CJ waved at the waiter and another cold bottle was brought for Eric. Amanda hoped Eric would spill everything he knew.

She leaned forward as though she was anxious, but she had no plans of stopping CJ from what he was doing.

"What's this boy's name?"

"Austin."

"Do you have his number? An address?"

Eric laughed. "Ah, even if I do. The boy pays *na*. The boy pays."

CJ brought out a bundle of two-hundred-naira notes and pushed it to Eric. The pimp pocketed it.

"Do you have paper and biro?"

CJ sniffed. "Just say everything."

Amanda stared at CJ. Eric opened his phone and called out two numbers. Then he brought out a small old diary and called out an address in Abuja. When the other guy was done, he put his diary back.

CJ didn't move. "Tell me about Austin."

"He said he wanted girls for a party on Sunday night. He was going to pay hundred-hundred dollars." Eric finished his second bottle.

CJ had the waiter bring a carton and drop beside Eric. "Keep talking," he told Eric.

After another hour, Eric was drunk and had probably said more than he should. CJ called the waiter and paid, then he helped Eric to his feet and led him to the car he rented from the hotel.

"Take me to the club," Eric said in a slurred voice.

"Of course," CJ said.

Instead, he drove toward the city gate, while Eric dozed off at the back seat.

Amanda scowled. "Do you know which club?"

"It won't matter."

The roads were busy but not enough to notice a man park his car by the bush and help his "friend" to pee. Only that CJ hit Eric and knocked him out the moment the other man opened his trousers. He removed the two bundles of money in his pockets and returned to the car.

Amanda gasped when he got back and pulled off without Eric. "What did you do to him?"

CJ shoved on his dark glasses though it was getting dark outside. "I took my money back. I may need it at Austin's."

"You didn't write down the address or number."

He called out both numbers and the address in the same order he was told. Amanda's mouth dropped open. She thought he must be a genius, but she couldn't afford to admire him more than she already did.

20

For several seconds CJ stared at Amanda's drooping lips, at the way her lovely eyes sucked him in, the way her chest rose and fell with her breathing, and he wasn't sure he could move. He tore his eyes away and put the car in drive.

"Thank you," she murmured. "You make this look so simple."

He swallowed. The only way he wanted her gratitude was with a kiss now and other things to follow. He blinked hard to focus.

"Eric never tells anybody anything. I had been wondering how we would break him because you never know what he knows."

He smirked. "He's a pimp, Amanda. Food, drink, and money, and he's singing. Like you saw today. That's why I wanted us to meet him at a joint, and not an office."

"That's very smart."

"I've been doing this job for over ten years. Besides, I was a crook myself." He chuckled. "I'm an insider."

She stole a glance at him. "What did you do?"

In his mind, he smiled. He could get her confessing to murder without her knowing but he realized she had never smiled around him. He wanted to see her smile and add another suffering to his pile. Each night he watched her sleep, he suffered. The night before, he had deliberately drunk more than was necessary to get over his desire. Seeing her come to him to go with her to see Nikky's brother had done him in. She didn't even know she "killed" him the more she depended on him. Her eyes, he knew, would one day drown him with the expectant expressions she probably wasn't aware of.

He chuckled aiming to amuse. "I stole meat from my mother's pot, for starters."

He checked his GPS and made a turn. He didn't know many places in Abuja, but the address was in the hinterland, extra-populated neighbourhoods the middle-to-low-class people lived.

"My mother didn't have a pot of her own. You steal from my step-mother's pot and you're dead."

"Did you ever try it?"

They got to a red light and he stopped. It was a good opportunity to stare at her. She twisted her fingers on her laps and stared out into the evening.

"Do you want to talk about it?"

She shook her head.

The lights changed and he moved on. "In secondary school, I started drinking, smoking, testing with women. That's a lot of criminal activity for an eleven-year-old." He sniffed. "I got good at it too."

"Do you still smoke? Because you got drunk last night, and I think you still like women."

He laughed. She didn't even smile or look at him, he realized from his blind-view. "I smoke sometimes. I drink sometimes. I womanize sometimes. I have no habits. I do what I like when I like."

"Good for you."

"I work all the time. That's my habit." He leaned a little toward her side. "What number do you see there?" He pointed at a story building on her side of the road.

She turned to it. "17."

"We're almost there. Going to 11."

She gasped. "It looks like 11."

"The numbers are not organised." He slowed and found parking by a small gutter. "I'm just going to call ahead."

He dialled the first number. "Switched off. The bane of crime." He dialled the second and got someone. "Yeah, I'm looking for Austin. I understand he's got a party coming and..." He paused. "Sure. Yeah, Eric gave me your number." He paused. "I'm outside. Not sure it's 17 or 11." He smirked. "Sure, coming in. Thanks." He hung up. "He says we should come in. He thinks I'm a pimp. We'll play that hand, okay?"

She nodded.

Inside the building had a winding staircase just short of the entrance and they took it. CJ knocked on the door and a young man opened the door. The sitting room they entered was furnished with suede upholstery with floral patterns. A 64" TV bracketed to the wall faced the front door, and a musical video played on it. The medium-sized room was well-lit with white lights, which added some form of beauty to the room. The young man motioned them to the couch. CJ put his age at twenty-five.

"Hi. I'm Austin. You came at the right time." He looked at Amanda. "You have only one girl?"

"I have more coming. Just wanted to be sure of the venue." CJ bit down on his jaw. "Changing room?"

"Let's talk figures first. How many girls and how much are you taking?"

CJ frowned. He had never been a pimp, but he dealt with some in the past. Pimps did not negotiate with other pimps and this "Austin" didn't quite fit the person Eric talked about. Austin was supposed to be much older, rich and in charge. The fidgety boy didn't add up.

CJ narrowed his eyes. "Where's Austin?"

The boy laughed. "What do you mean?"

"I asked you a question and I'm not here for play. I want Austin."

"Austin travelled but we handle everything." He shifted. "You don't need to fear, we will pay. Just tell me how much you will take."

CJ leaned back. "Give me the details and I will give you a cost. I told you I've not worked with Austin before. Eric told me about you people."

"Per one is five thousand. Up to four on one. Animal, we'll pay ten."

CJ burst into laughter. "Are you joking? *Abeg*, give me Austin's number, let me speak with him."

"He will tell you the same thing." He called out a number. "I can show you the changing room, if you agree."

"Show me. I will call Austin." CJ stood. "What's your name?"

"My name no mean."

He walked out the door and CJ followed him, followed by Amanda. Through a long corridor with closed doors on both sides, he stopped in front of the last and opened a small room with an adjoining bathroom.

"Nameless, leave us. I will call Austin and return to you in the parlour soon."

"No *wahala*." The boy left.

CJ arched his eyebrow. "Decode. What's four on one? Four girls on a guy?"

Amanda looked away. "Four guys on a girl."

CJ cursed. "And animal?"

"I don't know what that means."

"They put an animal on a girl?" He swore more violently and kicked a stool out of his way. "Did you ever *eff* a dog?" She did not reply, and he turned on her. "Answer me, damn you!"

"No. I never *effed* a dog. And I never did a four on one!"

21

—·—

CJ thought he was going to burn the building down. He had never been exposed to such treachery. Yet, the more he looked around the changing room, the more disgusted he was about the whole thing. Nikky had been here, with a dog or some other animal, he had no idea. And even if she wasn't, these guys had no conscience about subjecting university kids to gang-rapes. He trembled as he scrutinized the room, checking behind the curtain, and in the wardrobe, looking for what-he-had-no-idea.

He noticed Amanda trembled as well, dashing out of his way as he swung around the room after his outburst. He wasn't a man given to uncoordinated speech but the mere thought of the business going on here set him off. He opened the curtain and peeped out the window. Outside, the street was busy, cars moved up and down the road, honking and the world going on normally while a trade so debasing, he couldn't even fathom it was going on up here. He closed the curtain. On a dressing table, with a full-length mirror, he saw different personal care products for men and women. He picked a gel and read the details on it.

"Men use this room as well?" He gasped. "Have you ever been here before?"

"No."

Relief swept over him. "But Nikky came here!" He snapped.

He opened the door and peeped. Then walked to the closed door opposite the changing room. There were sounds from inside. He pressed his ear to the door.

"What are you doing? Did you call Austin?" Nameless shouted from the other end of the corridor.

CJ leaned against the door. "Are my girls here?"

"Not yet." The boy walked towards him. "Why are you there?"

"Because I want to check out your rooms. You think I will just let my girls inside here anyhow?"

"That room is occupied, Mr. CJ."

"Well, show me an empty room!" CJ frowned. "And how did you know my name?"

He snickered. "Your name showed on the phone when you called."

CJ *tsked*. He had that app and truly Austin's name had popped up on the two calls he made earlier.

"Cool. And stop using a number registered to Austin's name. So, empty room."

"I don't have any empty room. You have to wait."

"Okay, Nameless. We'll wait." He turned to enter the changing room.

"In the parlour. When these people finish, they will need the room to change."

"And we will leave it for them. Please, excuse me." CJ entered the room and slammed the door behind him.

Amanda jumped. He stared at her, his heart pounding in frustration at the mere thought of what she'd done with her body. How jealous he felt just thinking about it. All those nameless faces who had access to her body for peanuts! Five thousand for up to four on one! He could puke. And Nikky had followed the sneaky Austin for a hundred dollars. He could only imagine how many they put on her, man and dog! A hundred dollars! When she had access to his bank account...he wanted to weep. What could drive such a girl to such madness?

"There are people in this place already. I heard grunts in the opposite room." He paced. "I'm going crazy here, crazy."

"Maybe we should leave," she said softly. "I shouldn't have involved you in this mess."

He stopped moving and glared at her. "Why would you say that?"

"I disgust you, don't I?" She faced him. "I am a prostitute of the worst kind and just looking at me...it's as if you should kill me. I quite understand." She swallowed. "I deserve everything I get from you, the police, Nikky's family, Slopo. Everyone." She exhaled. "You don't owe me anything, and I think we should leave here. Return to Lagos tomorrow."

He walked towards her and expected her to move out of his way or flinch. She just stood there and waited for him to do whatever he planned. Her lips trembled to betray her courage and something in his belly dropped. He wanted to protect her from the life she had known, and for that brief moment, he didn't care if she'd had sex with a horse. He gripped her face and drew her into him. She struggled wildly, kicking at him, resisting his embrace, his impending kiss. He realized she was no longer that girl who did all those things and right now she could die protecting her integrity. It was easy to overpower her but when he did, he only held her, pressed her head into his chest as she wailed.

It lasted for several minutes then she calmed, and he murmured. "I'm not bailing on you, Amanda." He heaved. "Now pull yourself together and let's find Nikky."

She stepped back. "Thank you." And wiped her nose.

He walked to the door and pressed his ear against it. "I'm going to cause mayhem here, you just follow anything I ask of you."

She nodded. He winked, hoping to make her relax but her lips remained pressed tightly and her shoulders straight. He opened the door, motioned her to follow him, and knocked loudly on the opposite door.

Someone shouted, "Cut!" From inside. Paused. Then shouted. "*Wetin na, Oloriburuku!* We no go finish this shoot." After another moment's pause, he shouted. "Continue."

CJ could feel heat cover him. He touched his gun in his back pocket and took calming breaths. At this point, he knew he needed control, or he'd be guilty of murder. He placed his index finger on his lips as he saw the nameless boy run into the corridor.

"What is your problem, CJ? Why are you–?"

CJ pulled out his gun and pointed it at the boy. "What's your name?"

The boy raised his hands up. "Don't kill me, please. Ahhh, police."

"Your. Name."

"They call me James. Please. I'm just a houseboy. Please."

"James." CJ put his finger on his lips again. "Ssh. Now, come and tell them to open the door."

"*Oga*, please. They are shooting blue film, please."

"I'll shoot your legs. Don't let me ask two times."

James moved to the door and knocked. "*Abeg*, they said you should open. They want to pay. *Oga* wants to go."

The door jerked open before he could finish speaking. "What is your problem, you this–?" A stocky man stepped back mid-sentence when CJ pushed James into the room, the gun to his head.

CJ murmured. "Babe, take my phone from my pocket and do a video."

Amanda hesitated but did as he said quickly while the people in the room re-assembled, crouched, froze and reacted in different ways. CJ counted nine including the cameraman and someone holding a halogen lamp. Four naked men and one girl lay on the bed, with two young men, seemingly taking a break smoked weed on a couch.

"What's going on here, you bastards?" CJ panted. "Get dressed all of you. You're going to the station with me. You bloody bastards!"

They scrambled to dress up. CJ tried to grab the cameraman's camera but someone he had not seen surfaced from behind a door and shot at him. The bullet flew over his ear, and he thought it might have hit Amanda. Spontaneously, he shot in the ceiling. Amanda screamed.

"Amanda, go out, out!"

Despite himself, he held tight to James and dragged him out and kicked the door shut behind him. A door he suspected could be for emergency exit was the only one facing the long corridor, so he opened it. He was right. He gave way for Amanda to go first, down a flight of stairs, and then followed her, dragging James with him. He was in for a shocker downstairs. There was no exit door by the staircase. A door led to a long corridor, and at the end of it was the front door, and the stairway by it. And right by the stairway, three men with guns, leaned against the wall, in-waiting.

"We're trapped," CJ said. He shook James. "Is there another way to leave?"

"If we run across to the kitchen. Back door *dey*. Please don't kill me. I'm just a messenger."

CJ whispered harshly. "Where's the kitchen?"

"Just down there. Before the stair." James wept. "They go see us o."

"I will hold the gun on your head. They won't kill you—"

"They will shoot me. They will think I bring police, please!"

Amanda took off her blouse and pulled down a bra hand, exposing one full breast. She unzipped her jeans.

CJ barked between his teeth. "What are you doing?"

"They won't kill me. Hold the gun to my head, please!" She took off her jeans and his gaze followed her hips down. Sweat broke out on his forehead. "Let him go. Hold the gun to my head and let's find the kitchen." She snapped.

When he did not move, she snatched James out of his grip, put his hand on her head and walked forward. James scrambled back up the stairs. Amanda whimpered aloud and the three guys turned, their guns cocked.

"Please, please, don't kill me." She cried. "Please!"

CJ knew he'd eat his own bullet if she got killed. "Step back! All of you!" He yelled. "If you don't, she's dead."

It was the worst uncalculated risk he had taken in his life. One of the men hesitated and another shouted at him to back down. He found the kitchen door and pushed into it instead. What if there had been no kitchen, or it was locked? He'd die first. The back door was as James had mentioned but it didn't lead into the street but rather a walled compound. The idiot had fooled him into another trap. A badly damaged jeep was parked on one side, and a shed on the other. CJ ran with Amanda to the smashed vehicle and crouched. The dust-and-stone ground reminded him of her state of undress, and he pulled off his T-shirt, thankful it was one of the longer ones. His clothing on her made him yearn for another time, another place.

One of the men with the gun exited as they had and shouted. "The girl no be your *wahala*, let her go."

CJ snuggled closer, scratching his hairy chest on the sand, and bowed his head close to hers. "I'm sorry. I messed up. If he wants to kill me—"

There wasn't a lot of space between the jeep and the wall and they were forced to cuddle. He covered her with his body as much as he could.

"I will let them do anything to me before I let them kill you," she whispered.

He closed his eyes. "Do you know I have a crush on you? My last wish is to sleep with you."

"Stop talking like that."

"What's your full name?"

She giggled. His wish come true, just that he only heard the soft sound and didn't see her face.

"Amanda Chinasa Obi."

He moaned. "You're Ibo?"

"Yes. And you, what's your name?" She didn't let him talk. "CJ Christian Junior?"

He smiled. "Chetachukwu Jayamma Okondo. CJ is my initials."

Their hunter growled a foot away. "Stand up, idiot, before I blow your head into pieces!"

Amanda pushed back before CJ could stop her and looked up into the torch gleaming into her eyes.

"Chinasa!"

She sucked in her breath. "Emeka!"

22

Amanda couldn't be petrified being sandwiched between two men with guns. CJ clutched his handgun and Emeka pointed a double barrel at her. She jumped on her brother's neck and burst into tears for many reasons.

"Chinasa." Emeka groaned. "Oh, my father in heaven." He put her aside briefly and raised his gun at CJ. "You're a dead man."

"No!" Amanda threw herself between them. "He's my boyfriend. Calm down."

Emeka frowned. "Your boyfriend how? He had a gun to your—"

CJ lifted himself off the ground. "We need to get out of here." Nobody approached but it was a matter of time.

Emeka glanced around. "Come."

He led the way to the back of the shed. Part of the fence was broken down, and they climbed over it. No one would have discovered it unless someone who knew because all of the walls on that side was covered with brush. Through a bush path, they ran and burst into a small street. Emeka continued with the urgency of the moment and wove his way around several small streets.

He stopped at the back of a house. "If you continue in between all these houses straight, you'll burst out on the highway. You can call a taxi if you have money on you, or get a bus going to town."

Amanda grabbed his hand. "Please, come with us."

"Of course not!" Emeka gasped. "I have to get back. And you need to run. One or two of those guys know this path I followed. And they will soon come if they don't see me."

"That's why you need to come with us." Amanda clung to him. "Emeka, please. I won't go unless you come. Please."

"You never change, Chinasa. I will follow you, no problem." He led the way again.

Within minutes, they were on the highway as he'd said. They got an empty taxi willing to take them back to the hotel in Wuse at a crazy amount. CJ agreed to pay. The three sat in the back and kept mum until they were dropped off. It wasn't until they were in the safe confines of the hotel room that Amanda noticed the two men had hidden their guns. She could only imagine what the taxi driver thought they were; definitely criminals on the run. She jumped on Emeka's neck again, and this time had tears in her eyes.

"This is my small brother, Emeka." She turned to CJ. "We haven't seen him in four years." She sniffed. "Ah, Emeka. This is where you are?"

CJ stretched his hand and shook Emeka. "I'm CJ."

"I don't even know where to start." Amanda heaved. "Mama was so distraught. She fell sick for months."

"I think we all need to freshen up, I know I do. And I need a good meal." CJ cleared his throat. "I'll order food from the hotel."

"Is it not too late?" Amanda looked around, hoping to get an idea of time.

"It's close to 1am. But the kitchen here is always open." He walked to the telephone. "Anyone up for a heavy meal? And some strong drink?"

Amanda raised her hand. "No alcohol, please."

CJ smirked. "No alcohol. You can have the bathroom first, Amanda."

Amanda nodded. "Thank you."

She hurried off, hoping the men would not get into a fight. What a night but if there would be a wager on who would most likely cause trouble, she put it on CJ. A quick thought of those couple minutes before Emeka found them behind the wrecked jeep made her skin tingle. She didn't know if she looked forward to the conversation she'd eventually have with CJ about it.

They sat over pounded yam and oha soup in the sitting room part of the suite, at that ungodly hour, and none spoke until they were done eating. Amanda took the plates to the cart and returned to sit on the couch with Emeka. CJ leaned against the wall and opened up the conversation.

"Emeka, please we need answers. And I promise I will not implicate you in any way."

Emeka glanced at Amanda. "Is he a policeman?"

"No. He's Nikky's boyfriend."

Emeka frowned. "I thought you said he was your boyfriend."

She swallowed. "I said so just at that moment to stop you from killing him."

Emeka didn't seem convinced. "So, what answer do you want?"

"Where is Nikky? One Eric directed us to that house. Austin's house and see what goes on there." CJ paused. "Was Nikky in one of those rooms?"

Emeka grunted. "Hmm, Nikky." He regarded Amanda but rested his gaze on CJ. "First, Austin is dead."

Amanda gasped. "What?"

"Why am I not surprised!" CJ moaned. "Nikky?"

Emeka ran his ten fingers through his short brother locks. "I don't know. Look, this past month has been so scary."

Amanda tried to assimilate everything. She caught a glimpse of CJ, his brows drawn. He had an expression she couldn't read and wondered what was going on in his mind. She had to say something but didn't know what. The silence stretched. Emeka dropped his head to his chest and CJ glared at him with that strange look.

"What happened with you?" she whispered. "You just disappeared."

Emeka raised his head and his eyes were strained. "I needed to leave. You know how things were at home."

"But you should have told me at least."

"I told Nikky." Emeka sighed. "In fact, she gave me Austin's number. Said Austin was looking for a bodyguard." He slouched. "Well, Austin's boss."

He had always had well-toned muscles and at some point, worked at a local gym before it was raided and the owner carted away on drug-related charges. Emeka had spent a month in jail and after he came out was so depressed. He roamed the streets for another few months looking for a job and then disappeared.

CJ spoke, "Do you know what happened to Austin? How he died?"

For a long moment, Emeka just hugged his arms around himself, and Amanda reached over and patted his back. When he could speak, he gazed into space.

"This Austin guy was just a go-between. Ordinary hustler. They dress him up, give him car, make him look like something, meanwhile, the boy sleeps in the BQ like all of us." He kissed his teeth. "The boss opened one house in Lokoja." He swallowed. "Austin was coming back when they had accident." He pointed toward the door. "That jeep you people hide behind is the one they had the accident with." He ruffled his hair again. "Ah, Austin did not even get a proper burial. They just hide their bodies in one small grave with the other girl. Telling everybody Austin is still in business." He bit his fingers and dropped his head again.

Amanda gasped. "Oh, dear Lord!"

CJ's voice was so cold, it froze the room. "What other girl?"

"The girl in front." Emeka shuddered. "They will give him dollar he cannot spend for himself. Meanwhile, his poor mother is there."

CJ clenched his teeth. "Not Nikky. Another girl?"

Emeka shook his head, and Amanda released her breath. It still did not explain Nikky's whereabouts but at least, there was a little hope. She closed her drooping eyes, but they popped open when CJ suggested they rested for the night.

"Amanda can have the room. Emeka and I will crash here," he said to no one in particular.

23

Neither man moved and both watched Amanda walk into the adjoining bedroom and close the door. CJ's heart thudded with need. He should be following her inside to hold and comfort her after such a near-death experience. He still couldn't believe how fast things escalated. How steep their escape had been. Never in his imagination had he thought they were stepping into a den of criminals, or that he would lose control of his wit so fast, and though Emeka was speaking in staccatos, he needed to get as much as he could from him.

"The bar is open twenty-four hours." He stared at the young man's bent head. "Do you want anything?"

Emeka raised his head. "Bitters."

CJ nearly laughed. The boy was so crude, but he understood a strong drink would only do anyone some good. He called the bar and ordered Emeka's drink. He knew the boy would talk more if they both had drinks but a nudge about Amanda's deference stopped him and he got nothing for himself. When the barman left, he checked his decision again and knew he had to have an important conversation with Amanda. She already affected him and his near-death confession to her made him hot all over.

"I guess you are reluctant to give details of what happened, but your sister needs your help." CJ watched the younger man with hooded eyes. "Nikky's mother sent the police to arrest her."

Emeka lowered the small bottle of bitters from his mouth. "Why?"

"I'm sure you know their relationship. Nikky's mother believes she handed Nikky over to Amanda."

"Are you here for Nikky or for Chinasa?" Emeka lay his head on top of the couch. "You stare at my sister as if you want to eat her up." He closed his eyes.

"I think I'm in love with her." CJ chuckled. "You see how foolish I am? And you have to help me find Nikky. For Amanda's sake."

Mentally he rolled his eyes. He knew about patronizing young people who thought they were wise. He was entering grill-mode and if Emeka didn't speak up, he'd use his worst weapons of manipulation. He hoped he didn't have to.

Emeka grunted. "I told Nikky. I warned her." He opened one eye. "Heaven knows where she is. Because I don't."

CJ stared at the empty bottle of bitters dangling from Emeka's hand. He would be knocked out in a minute, but he will talk. Even if he had to force the words out of his mouth.

"She called you from Lokoja. What did she say?"

Emeka groaned again. "Man, can we do this tomorrow? Wait." He raised his head. "How do you know she called?"

"Because I got her phone records. I'm not joking here, bro. I didn't come here to gaze at Zuma rock, or whatever you people have here. I dialled every number I saw on her records and your name popped up." CJ walked over and crouched in front of him. "Talk to me. What did Nikky tell you when she was in Lokoja?" He breathed hard. "She called your number four times. Sent a text once."

Emeka's throat worked up and down. CJ could see he wasn't drunk or drowsy. He just didn't want to talk, but he had to.

He blinked bloodshot eyes. "This is what happened. Austin offered hundred dollars each to come and do blue movie. When the thing finished, the boss asked anyone who wants to come to Lokoja. Just for one night to do another one. He will pay hundred thousand naira each." He sighed. "I told Nikky not to go because that Lokoja, I've been there before. Some girls die doing that thing. And they just throw their body inside the confluence. But the money entice Nikky."

CJ registered everything in his brain. All he could think of was getting another car to drive to Lokoja. Now.

"I make her promise she will call me when she get there and if there is problem." Emeka swallowed hard. "She called. The last one, she said they want to kill her. That she has not rest for eight hours and they never finish. I tell her to speak to one guy, a cameraman, named Desmond. That he will help her leave the place."

When he didn't say any more for several minutes, CJ prompted him softly. "And?"

"Her text. Came the following day around 5pm." He blinked. "I'm dying, help me." He shuddered. "I called Nikky. Called and called, her number didn't go through. I called Desmond, what is going on? Desmond say he's not there, he don't know. When a girl die like that, they destroy everything she come with. I was afraid Nikky die and they dispose her."

CJ let this sit for several more minutes as he processed the information. The following day would be Monday, he gathered.

"How many of the girls went?"

"Three," Emeka said. "With Austin driving."

"There's still a girl missing. She and Nikky did not return?"

"I don't know." Emeka closed his eyes again. "Nobody is saying anything. Lokoja people and the boss here are all saying nothing happened. That the girls all left and arrived safely. But we know Austin had accident and only two bodies were found. Because *na* we find and bring back the jeep."

"How?"

Emeka grunted. "We tow with our own jeep."

CJ stared into the space above Emeka's head. There was only one way to find out if Nikky left. To go to Lokoja. He wasn't ready to risk what happened earlier again so he would not wake Amanda up. It was barely 4am and he hadn't slept in eighteen hours, but this had to be done now. When they were well on their way, he'd call Amanda and let her know what they were up to. She would just have to wait until they returned. He would not be rash and pull out his gun this time, and he needed to have a proper plan. He'd discuss one with Emeka on the way.

He focused on Emeka. "We need to go to Lokoja. Now. I'll get a car and we'll drive."

Emeka sneered. "You and who?"

Amanda stood between the connecting doors. "Three of us."

24

— · —

The two men turned at the same time. Amanda folded her arms across her chest, ready to challenge any opposition to her statement. She knew Emeka would not want to go with CJ and CJ did not want to go with her. They all had to go. She wasn't going to allow them to leave her pacing and panting, dying of anxiety.

CJ leaped to his feet and approached her. When he got to her, he backed her into the room and closed the door.

"I'm not going to risk your life again like what happened earlier." He snapped. "And you have nothing to say about it."

She leaned on her toes so she would be nose-to-nose with him. "I am coming with you, and you have nothing to say about that."

Immediately she spoke she realized just how tempting the posture was. She wanted to kiss him, and his gaze dropped to her lips. Too late she stepped back but his hand was already in the small of her back. She flipped her face away just in time to avoid his lips, which caught her earlobe.

CJ moaned. "Amanda, please. Please."

His hand roamed her body, drawing her into him. She didn't know what he was pleading for. Was it to stay back or to kiss?

Her reply fitted both. "No, CJ."

She buried her face in his chest and held tightly to the front of his shirt, because it was the only way she could fight the urges within her, to succumb to his caress, his plea. To fight his searching mouth. He buried his hands in her hair and tried to make her look at him, but she dug in, afraid he would see the desire in her eyes, afraid her resolve would weaken if she saw the one in his.

"They could kill you." He growled. "See what almost happened tonight."

She wrapped her arms around his waist and hugged tight. She couldn't bear to have anything happen to him either and if it would happen, she had to be there with him.

"I'm not staying back."

They continued to hold each other until she could feel the tension ease from him. She relaxed her hold and stepped out of his embrace, but it wasn't until she was a safe distance away, and with some furniture in between them did she look at him.

"I'm begging you too. Besides, Emeka doesn't know you and he won't want to go with you alone."

CJ shook his head. "I meant what I said behind that jeep. I have a crush on you. In fact, I think I'm in love with you."

She was shaking her head before he could finish. "No, CJ."

"Yes. What are you afraid of? Look at how we fit each other?"

"I don't fit anybody." She swallowed. She had to come to terms with the truth. "Let's just find Nikky and go our separate ways."

He snickered. "You know that can't be the end. First, you have a case against you, and I'm your lawyer."

"You're not."

He shook his head. "You argue about everything. But it doesn't matter. I'm not going to disappear into thin air after all of this."

"Well, let's leave to Lokoja then. Afterward we can talk about...about other things."

He smiled. "Promise me we will talk about us, if I let you go to Lokoja."

She wanted to tell him he couldn't stop her. All she'd just do was convince Emeka not to go, but she could still feel the way his body vibrated against hers as he fought a need so strong as she'd never felt on a man before. It would bruise his ego after such a rejection.

She smiled too. "I promise."

He groaned. "You're even prettier when you smile, Amanda. Your face lights up the world."

She turned. "We need to get ready to leave now. There's no time to waste."

"If you're coming then you need to catch some sleep. We all need to."

She shook her head. "If I sleep now, I won't be able to wake up on time. And you guys may sneak off."

"We won't leave you. I promise."

She walked towards the door. "Let's discuss with Emeka then." She didn't know why she simply trusted him. He opened the door for her and for a moment, she feared he would touch her again, but he let her pass, panting.

25

—·—

When Amanda woke up alone on the king-size bed in the hotel room, she cursed herself for allowing CJ to talk her into sleep. She knew her body needed it but not at a time every minute counted. Before they left, CJ had made it clear he wanted to return to Lagos today to resume his work and normal life and she should never have agreed to "sleep a little." They had left her for Lokoja, surely!

She sat up straight, her heart thudding. What was she going to do now? She didn't have Emeka's number and he didn't have hers. She had to call CJ. They must turn around and come and pick her up. A single knock on the door brought her attention away from rummaging her ruck sack, searching for her phone.

"Wake up, babe," CJ said softly and knocked again.

"I'm awake!" She jumped off the bed and glared at herself, still wearing his T-shirt.

He opened the door slowly. "I'm coming in."

She leaped back on the bed. Her hair she knew would be ruffled and she didn't want to continue to be seen fully dressed in his clothing. It made her feel too vulnerable.

She rubbed her eyes and yawned. "What time is it?"

"You didn't sleep a lot. It's not yet nine." He leaned against the wall. "I got a car. Do you want breakfast?"

"No."

"I ordered sandwiches. I felt we should eat or at least take something with us."

"Makes sense."

He turned to leave. "We'll let you freshen up."

She coughed. "I don't have anything to wear."

"Really?" He chuckled. "I'll call reception. I think there's a boutique in the hotel."

"Size 8," she mumbled. "Thank you."

"My pleasure." He left.

She slumped back unable to believe how grateful she was they didn't leave her. He kept his word. Maybe that was the type of person he was, someone who would always keep his word. Men rarely did, and she liked him a tad more for that. They could have left and all she'd do was scream at no one but herself. She rushed into the bathroom and stood under the shower, allowing the water to calm her. Today was big, and scary and hopeful. Nikky must be found.

What CJ made out to look like mere breakfast was a banquet of sandwiches, fruits, snacks and drinks. Amanda exclaimed when she got into the rental car and saw the array set on the back seat.

Emeka laughed. "I asked him whether we're going for a party."

She sat on the small space left for her on the back and mumbled. "Thank you, CJ."

He started the ignition. "Well, we may need it, and if we don't, we have nothing to lose."

Emeka gave him an address and he put it into the car's GPS.

She stared at the device absently. "What will happen to the other car?"

"I told the rental I was attacked and had to abandon it." He shrugged when she gasped. "They have insurance." He snickered. "And a tracking device. They'll go and reclaim their car."

"Did you have to pay extra?" She wondered aloud.

He checked the road and pulled in. "They didn't give me my deposit back. Fine."

"It must be a risky business in this country," she muttered.

"There seems to be traffic leaving town but hopefully in three hours, we should be there," CJ said. "Did you let anyone know you're coming, Emeka?"

"I dare not. Boss would have heard what happened yesterday! They have call my number tire."

"Who are they?"

"Huh, Chinasa! You sure Nikky dated this guy that can ask question from heaven to earth?"

Amanda rested her head back and closed her eyes. She felt so tired despite at least four hours of good sleep. She just wanted all of this to pass.

CJ laughed. "I didn't have to ask Nikky questions." He heaved a heavy sigh. "Now I regret that."

Emeka chuckled. "Nikky will never tell you the truth."

Amanda wanted to let Emeka know CJ was skilled in the art of detecting lies but kept quiet. Let him try his luck.

"I know she lied about a few things. But her age! Dang, it. I don't know how I missed that." CJ paused. "So, who are *they*?"

"Colleagues," Emeka mumbled.

"Emeka, tell me how you ended up here," Amanda asked, her eyes still closed. "Then CJ will stop asking you questions you don't want to answer."

Emeka snickered. "How else? I told you I asked Nikky if she get friends that can get me a job and she sent me here."

She raised her head and opened her eyes. "Did she know the people? And the business they did? And why didn't you ask me!"

"Their business? I don't know. I never enter inside—"

"Stop lying, Emeka. I know what we saw inside there, and what that boy was saying." She sighed. "My only fear now is that they killed Nikky or she died, and they have thrown her away."

"I'm just wondering, though, Amanda." CJ cut in. "How come you didn't know your "missing" brother was in Abuja, on a job recommended by your roommate?"

She rolled her eyes. "I told you we don't have such discussions." When she glanced in his direction, she noticed he was staring at her through the rear-view mirror. She looked away.

"Nikky knew the kind of things these guys did, and introduced your brother to it?" CJ shook his head. "She knew you were worried about him too."

"She's missing now and it's my fault." She rubbed her forehead. "I guess I have to ask you questions now, Emeka. The people you work for—"

"I will protect you, Emeka. I know this can be worrying and you didn't want to come for this trip," CJ said softly. "But we need to know what we are going to face in Lokoja. Or do you want your sister to be exposed to danger like yesterday?"

Emeka scratched his head, obviously struggling with the decision to speak or not. "See, I'm dead as it is. Those other guys saw me leave with you."

Amanda leaned forward and touched his shoulder. "CJ is a lawyer and a very good one too. You can trust him." She lowered her voice. "I do. I owe my life to him."

She looked in the mirror, knowing he would too, and their gazes held a second long enough for her stomach to drop.

"My boss." Emeka groaned. "My boss is...is Chief... Aruruala."

Amanda tore her eyes away from CJ and exclaimed. "The Chief Kalu!"

"Yes." Emeka nodded. He scratched his head. "I'm a dead man."

26

—·—

The traffic out of town wasn't as bad as CJ had envisaged and soon, they were on the freeway. Since Amanda stepped out of the hotel clad in the red Polo T-shirt and black jeans he bought her in the hotel boutique, he hadn't been able to breathe normally. The outfit gripped her figure as though she was tailored into it, exposing just how curvy and beautiful she was. He had gotten several outfits, but she had chosen this, and he envisaged what she'd look like in the others. And with the way she constantly met his gaze in the mirror, rolled her eyes, leaned back, pouted, and stretched, he couldn't wait for the day to be over and to get away from her. No woman had ever made him feel so lustful, and she shunned him every chance he got to touch her. She was playing a dangerous game with him. He had never had his patience stretched so far.

"CJ, the man is—"

"I know Chief Kalu. Nicknamed the wicked one. Kearuruala!" He sighed. "My legal success began when I won a case for him nine years ago."

"Huh, so you're the reason he's free to do all he does." Amanda screeched. "He's the godfather. You know that?"

"He had a case?" Emeka gasped. "The formidable, a court case?"

CJ laughed. "He was going to fall flat. The evidence against him was a mountain."

Amanda kissed her teeth. "Why did you defend him?"

"Because he paid me to." CJ felt a tinge of guilt. "Someone will anyway, and get almost ten million? Why not me? It was my first big job. Besides, in our profession, you are constrained to defend an accused except on religious grounds."

"I'm just wondering why he'd use you. You said it was your first big job," Emeka asked.

"My first big job, but not my first. I had a track record of never losing my cases. And the really big lawyers didn't want him because he was too politically...should I say, entangled? I was young and had no strings attached."

Amanda asked. "Would you take him on now?"

"I'm still politically unattached. And now I have a reputation. I take on the worst criminals."

She exclaimed. "Don't you have any conscience?"

He swallowed and caught her gaze in the mirror. She wanted to kill him, obviously. Because she clenched her teeth. He looked back at the road. "The money is good."

"Blood money," she muttered.

"If it makes you feel better." CJ barked. "I get drunk after some of those cases!" A tense silence followed. "This is not about the money, if that makes you feel better." He sighed. "I just said that to annoy you. Every man is presumed innocent until proven guilty."

Amanda spat. "Nonsense!"

Emeka coughed. "Guy, calm down. Aruruala's case will get anybody drunk."

CJ frowned. "Who are you calling in Lokoja? Let's have a plan."

"I can't call anybody until we get there, CJ. I don't want somebody to be waiting for me." Emeka replied.

"Makes sense," CJ said. "All the same, we can have a plan. Do you know where Chief Kalu is now?"

"He dey Abuja," Emeka mumbled.

"Can you tell us what business goes on where we're going?"

Amanda cut in before Emeka could answer CJ's question. "What was Aruruala's offense when you defended him?"

CJ sucked in his breath. "Child sacrifice. Three count."

She cursed like he'd never heard her before.

****

The rest of the journey progressed in near-silence, with CJ asking just a few questions and Emeka's reluctant responses. Amanda dozed off, which made CJ extremely relieved. No one touched the food. Her anger at him when she got to know the criminal he'd defended hurt deeper than he expected. This was his job. Even his family never questioned the morality behind what he did, and why would she? What moral pedigree did she have to question his profession when she sold her body and recruited others to do as well. Still, pangs of guilt hit every angle on his inside. Chief Kalu should have been hung by now. He had won the case on a clever technicality. The evil man would not be alive to boss anyone or run a brothel and shoot dreadful ex-rated movies.

CJ had never visited Lokoja but while at the hotel, he had done his background check. The small confluence city was also the state capital but purely an agricultural town and basically sleepy by his own assessment. Development was not much. A typical Nigerian city with everything on the slow side of the clock. CJ understood why it would be easy to set up a business sourced from Abuja, just two hundred kilometres away.

Entering the town, the road was bad, and this incredibly slowed down the journey. The GPS took them to the middle of a busy street a lot like the one in Abuja. CJ parked between an old saloon car and a broken-down lorry.

"We're here, what next?"

Emeka fidgeted. "Let me call someone and find out if they are inside."

CJ looked up and down the street. The buildings were old and a mix of shops, bungalows, and story buildings. Typical of a street in a Nigerian town.

"Which house are we talking about here?"

Emeka nodded toward a general direction, which made no sense, but he dialled a number on his phone. He turned away from CJ and muffled his voice enough so no one in the car would hear him.

CJ looked back at Amanda who'd been unusually quiet since she cursed at him. "Are you okay?"

She nodded. Emeka finished the call and turned to him.

"So, here's what's happening. I just called one of the girls who live in town. She said she hasn't been here for about a month."

CJ arched his eyebrow. "And?"

"She doesn't really know what's going on—"

"Emeka, call someone inside the house. Or show me, and I'm going in." CJ snapped. "Amanda, you'll stay in the car on inside that shop selling drinks." He pointed. "Over there."

"Will you be patient and let him talk?" She said quietly.

Her words jolted him, and he folded his arms across his chest. "Emeka doesn't want to talk. Maybe you can make him."

"I don't know what we're doing here." Emeka scratched his head. "These people don't care. They will kill you right here on the street and nothing will happen."

Amanda leaned forward. "Can we speak to the shop owners or neighbours?"

"If they know anything, they won't tell." Emeka glared at CJ. "You saved a monster and he has grown bigger."

"Huh, give me a break. When the police round them all up, I'm going to be defending you and you will be thanking me." CJ paused. "Next steps, we can't just sit here."

Amanda exhaled. "Emeka, is there anyone else you can call, please?"

"The girl I called, she was at the house during that weekend."

CJ snapped. "Why didn't you say so since? Where does she live?"

He didn't wait for Emeka to respond. He put the car in gear and smoothly piloted the car back on to the road.

"She won't talk unless you give her some money."

Amanda responded before CJ could. "He'll give her."

27

—·—

Chomi's house was located downtown on the other side of town, and CJ hoped they would not need to go elsewhere afterward. He had his secret fears about exposing Amanda to danger like the day before. The question kept thumping in his heart, "What if the gunman who came after them was not Emeka?" At the time, he had known they were in danger but after realizing *Kearuruala* was on top of this, it could have gone either way. If they were patient enough to take him to their boss, they'd be saved but he knew that in most of these circumstances, the "boys" were more wicked than their master and took action without sense.

An elderly woman opened the door for them and led them through a short corridor to a badly lit room. CJ couldn't help but notice the strong stench of a rotting wound bathed in iodine. The place smelt worse than a dirty clinic. Emeka entered first, followed by Amanda and he came in, for a moment, feeling for his gun safely tucked away in his back pocket. Though it had almost backfired yesterday, he was ready to use it at a second's notice. He noticed the young woman on the single bed immediately. The room had a chair pushed against the wall to the side facing the bed. A double window with a light-coloured curtain covering it was open but did little for the ventilation. Neither did a ceiling fan blowing at full-speed.

Emeka hurried to the woman's side. "Chomi, you sick?" He looked around. "Where this?"

Chomi drew in a shaky breath. "My grandmother house." Her gaze went to CJ and Amanda who stood closer to the door than the bed. "Who be them?"

"My sister, Chinasa, and her, her friend, CJ." He waved to them. "Their other friend, Nikky was at the hotel with you that weekend."

Chomi closed her eyes and turned to one side. "I no get what to tell you, Emeka. I talk that one for phone now."

"I will pay for any information you can give on Nikky, please." CJ took a step forward, standing beside Amanda.

"I no know who Nikky is. Girls dey plenty."

The old woman came to stand at the door. "She no well o, she no well o."

"Mama, is-s-okay. I fine," Chomi mumbled. "Go, *abeg*." Grumbling, the woman left.

CJ dipped his hand in his jean pocket and pulled out a bundle of five hundred Naira notes. "Here's 5k."

Chomi turned to him slowly. "Give Mama. She need am more than me."

Emeka took the money and left the room. CJ took a step closer, and this time, he held Amanda's hand and brought her closer.

"What happened at the hotel that weekend five weeks ago?"

Chomi smirked. "They say *na* 100k for the show. From morning till night. All night, the following day. They bring one animal which resemble goat. Dog too. At last, they pay fifty. The girls begin quarrel. The ones from Abuja leave angry."

CJ cut in. "Nikky was one of the ones from Abuja."

"I don't know their name. Three or four of them leave with one man." Chomi sighed. "As I was saying, so we here start to shout for our complete money. Boys come inside and beat us. Throw us out." She sighed. "Since then, I sick. I come my grandmother place to take care of me."

CJ noticed tears trickled down her face. "Did you go to the hospital? You seem very sick."

"I go the hospital. They say my under *don* spoil. Call money for surgery wey I not get. Even the 50k they give, I use more than half for test." She swallowed. "That *na* why I come here. My grandmother *na* herbal doctor."

"How much for the surgery?"

Chomi scoffed. "Two-fifty."

CJ looked at Amanda and noticed there were tears in her eyes too. "When Emeka comes, I think we should take her to the hospital. I'll pay for the surgery."

Amanda gasped and grabbed his neck to his surprise. Her hug was big and brief, but he could feel her in every part of his body.

Emeka returned. "Mama thinks we should leave. She wants to clean Chomi's wound."

Amanda gushed. "We're taking her to the hospital. She needs surgery and CJ wants to pay for it."

Emeka exclaimed. "Ah, God bless you, sir."

CJ nodded. "I think we need an ambulance. And I need to get to a bank."

28

— · —

CJ paid for an ambulance, and Chomi was taken to the emergency room immediately and scheduled for surgery as soon as they could get her test results in. A resident doctor walked over to them in the waiting room afterward.

"Are you her family?"

Emeka nodded and Amanda nodded. CJ shook his head.

"Well, please follow me." The doctor motioned to Emeka and Amanda.

"Actually, we're just her friends," Amanda said. "He's, my friend." She looked at CJ. "He's paying. None of us live here."

The doctor exclaimed. "Well, does she have family around? Who will be here after her surgery?"

Emeka spoke. "I know her house. I think her sister use to live with her."

The doctor nodded. "It will be good to get someone who lives here to come. Can you do that?"

"Yes, doctor. We will find her family." Amanda looked at Emeka.

"Thank you. As soon as possible, please." He nodded again and walked away.

CJ got restless. Nikky was still missing and the sick girl had only given a small piece of the puzzle. "Can you call the sister? Or we have to drive somewhere again."

"We have to drive there, I don't have her number," Emeka said.

CJ marched towards the exit. "Is the girl your girlfriend?"

Emeka snapped. "No. She is my friend."

"Of course, she is," CJ muttered.

They finally got a hold of Chomi's older sister close to seven in the evening and had to decide whether to return to Abuja or spend the night or try and find the information about Nikky.

"Would you want to eat something?" Amanda asked softly.

"No, I can't get that stench in the old woman's house out of my gut!" CJ snapped. "Thanks, anyway."

"Me too. I'll have that smell in me for a week." She wiped imaginary sweat off her forehead. "Emeka?"

"I need to eat. Since morning, nothing." He opened the cooler and removed a beer. Amanda handed him an egg and tomato sandwich. "Thank you."

For several minutes no one said anything as they sat inside the car in the parking lot of the general hospital after dropping Chomi's sister off. CJ opened his phone and scrolled through tons of missed calls from the office, the police, private business concerns, Yemi, and just about everyone he knew. He closed all and checked out the messages, and emails. Just a day, and it seemed his life had fallen apart. He couldn't afford many more days like this.

He rested his head back on the headset and took deep breaths.

"Emeka, do you know anyone else you can talk to?" Amanda said soberly. "What about the cameraman you called when we were in the hotel."

Emeka finished the sandwich and took another. "Honestly, I just feel miserable." He chewed noisily. "This whole thing, I've just try not to involve myself."

Amanda patted his shoulder. "You always liked Nikky. And she helped you get this job."

Emeka shrugged her hand off. "She destroyed my life. See what I am doing now." He snapped. "She know I like her and see what she gave me. I will be in Lagos now, working another gym."

Amanda leaned back. "I think she was just trying to help you."

"And I tell her not to come here. These people have no conscience. See what happen to Chomi." Emeka hissed. "Nikky just like to play with somebody emotion."

"Now she's missing. Please, you need to help."

Emeka sighed. "In fact, if not for CJ and what he do Chomi. See, that girl dey rotten from inside." Emeka finished the second sandwich and gulped down his beer.

CJ raised his head and glared at him for a moment, then turned on the ignition. He was tired, and felt stinky, and just wanted to have a long bath, eat and sleep. Tomorrow was another day. He'd decide whether to dump Emeka and Amanda when he'd had time to think. While the siblings slept in the early hours of the morning, he'd been busy making calls, strategizing, planning for the trip to Lokoja and any eventuality with the criminal. He hadn't envisaged the day would go the way it did.

"At least she confirmed the Abuja people left," Amanda said.

Emeka reached to the back and grabbed another can of beer. "Truth is, is we that go to remove the jeep at the accident. But we see only Austin and the other girl inside."

"At least there should be someone you can call—" Amanda started.

"Wait." CJ raised his hand to cut her off. "Keep talking, Emeka."

Emeka finished that beer and reached to the back. Amanda slapped his hand off. "No more. You want to get drunk?"

Emeka belched. "Na so person drunk?"

CJ snapped. "Can you remember where you found the jeep?"

Emeka looked out and didn't speak for a long time. CJ inputted the trip to Abuja into the GPS. He wasn't going to waste any more time on this issue and if Emeka refused to cooperate, he would call in his team of policemen who had been on standby in Abuja and Lokoja all day and have him locked up until he was ready to talk. He pulled out to the road and had decided to go for plan B when Emeka spoke again, his deep voice low and cracking.

"Nikky tell me they were finally leaving. That text I say she send, is like she send it after the accident. Because when we go find the jeep. The accident already happen, and her text enter my phone. I first think she talk of inside the hotel. But even Austin confirm he leave with three Abuja girls and Nikky is one."

"I don't understand you, Emeka. If she left, how could she send a text after the accident?" Amanda moaned. "With that jeep so badly destroyed, she would be crushed if she was inside."

"Unless she was flung out, somehow, or rescued." CJ frowned. "Take us to where you found the jeep." He picked his phone and called his police contact in Abuja.

29

The accident occurred on the outskirts of Abuja, where a road construction had considerably narrowed the throughway. District Police Officer (DPO) Aliyu arrived with a handful of his officers in two vans, just as CJ pulled over by the side of the road. Before leaving the metropolis, he had bought six powerful torches with extra batteries. Emeka and Amanda had merely stared at him, their jaws dropping, as he moved in a frenzy. When he told them they all were conducting a search of the area, their eyes had popped, but apparently, they had no idea what a beast he became when he decided to embark on a task.

It was eleven o'clock, and the DPO had battery-powered halogen lamps with at least eight men. CJ clasped him in a side-hug.

"Thank you so much, DPO."

"Anytime, Barrister," Aliyu said in a heavily-accented voice. "Where is the man?"

"Emeka!" CJ called out and Emeka and Amanda moved closer. "Meet DPO Aliyu."

"Good evening, sir." Emeka scratched his head. "I don't want police *wahala*," he mumbled.

CJ arched an eyebrow. "Where did you pull the vehicle from?"

Emeka pointed. "This whole area. We pulled it out around here. We were driving for a long time before we find it."

Aliyu snickered. "Any police report?"

Emeka raised his hands in a gesture of surrender. "I just be messenger. My boss just said we should come here."

CJ patted Aliyu. "I'll check up on the report later. Let's just search now."

"No problem, Barrister." Aliyu raised his voice. "Go in. Constable Ignatus! Wait behind with the vehicles."

One of the policemen shouted, "Yes, sir."

Aliyu walked towards his men and divided them into three, because they had three strong lights.

CJ turned to Amanda. "You'll stay in the car with the constable."

"No." She burst out. "I'm not staying behind."

"I will stay," Emeka offered.

"You're coming with us, Emeka. And you, Amanda, will wait here. I'm not going to risk you getting in danger again."

She stood with arms akimbo. "Stop me if you can."

CJ pulled her aside. "You can't be stubborn now, Amanda. Please."

Amanda breathed heavily. "What about you? Are you not in danger? With all these policemen, you feel you can boss everyone around and do what you wish?"

He gasped. "I'm doing this for you. Don't you want to find Nikky?"

She shrugged off his hand which had remained on her arm. "Oh, please. You're doing it for yourself. You want to display how much power you have. Commanding people all over the world to do your bidding."

"I have people when I need people. How is that a bad thing?"

"It's a good thing if someone with the right motive is doing it."

"Come on, give me a break. I have my own crew of men in arms. Do you think it's easy to help gang leaders and drug barons take a walk?"

She hugged her waist. "You're as much a public enemy as they are."

"Thank you." He refused to challenge her right to accuse him. "Now, let's get back, they are ready."

Aliyu had the sirens turned on for the two police vehicles so anyone driving by would understand this was an official search, and other security personnel would not stop to investigate. CJ stayed close to Amanda, both had two torches on. Emeka lagged behind but had two sources of light too. The vegetation was dry and light, and this made it easy to comb through.

A couple of kilometres off the road, a stench so strong got them distracted. Amanda turned towards it and CJ tried to get in front of her to lead the way, but he stepped forward too late. She screamed and dropped her torches. CJ caught her in his arms as he saw the decaying corpse. For the first time in hours, he was grateful he'd not eaten because his insides protested at the image and the smell overwhelmingly in the air.

Emeka came forward quickly and turned just as fast.

"Blow the whistle," CJ murmured and carried a weeping Amanda away from there.

Aliyu had given everyone a whistle to alert others if anyone found anything.

Amanda struggled against him. "No. No."

"Calm down, honey," he cooed into her ear, walking as fast as he could.

She was lighter than he expected, or maybe he was just energized by the new pump of adrenaline in his blood. Emeka's whistle soon drew attention from all the other teams and the policemen ran towards them. Aliyu asked them to return to the vehicles and called for the emergency service to bring a vehicle to remove the corpse.

For another two hours, they waited in the car while a vehicle arrived and the rotting corpse was taken to a mortuary. Again, CJ made all the necessary payments though no one had identified the corpse. Close to six in the morning, the three stumbled back into the hotel room. CJ could hardly stand. He waited patiently until the siblings had used the bathroom, and then had a long bath. When he came out, feeling better refreshed, he found Emeka asleep on the couch, and Amanda cuddled in the single chair, hugging her feet.

"You should be in bed," he mumbled.

He hadn't slept in two nights and his head ached, to put his feeling mildly. He considered getting a second room, have a bed to himself, but he didn't want either Emeka or Amanda out of his sight, especially now.

"That was Nikky." She sobbed.

He walked over to crouch in front of her. "We don't know that yet."

"I know." She leaned over and hugged his neck and wailed. "I know."

CJ lifted her and took her into the bedroom, his heart thudding. It would be so easy to take advantage of her. He wanted to comfort her above all but there was no way his emotions would not get in the way. He placed her on the bed, and she clung to his neck.

"I'm not leaving you." He groaned. "You need to sleep, and me too. It's going to be a long day."

"Nikky. She was wearing my coral. My beads on her—" She heaved as though she'd puke. "Waist. I saw it. She stole it. I asked her about it." She took several seconds wailing.

CJ pressed her face into his shoulder and massaged her head and neck. "It's alright, darling. Stop crying, baby."

"She steals. Nikky was always stealing. From me." She lifted her head and stared at him. "And the last time I talked with her, I was quarrelling about my beads. And now she has died!"

CJ cupped her face. "It's okay. I understand."

Tears streamed from her eyes and nose. "I made her into the horrible person she became. I taught her everything she knew, and she came around to steal from me."

He wiped her tears with his bare hands. "You didn't know any better."

She sniffed. "I did. I hated her. She was prettier than me. All the boys wanted her."

CJ pulled her closer. "Don't do this to yourself, Amanda. You're tired you need to sleep."

"I tried to change her back. Preach to her. But she was too far gone." She burst into another bout of tears. "Oh, God forgive me. I didn't even want the boys." She sniffed. "I hated the boys. But I was so jealous of Nikky."

CJ thought it was better to let her release all her pain and sadness. Tears they say was therapeutic.

"You like me better than her, don't you?" She cried.

"I do. I like you way better," he said.

She gripped his face and kissed his mouth. "Thank you."

She kissed him again, and lingered, seeking to make him open his mouth. He knew what was going on and much as he wanted her so badly, he couldn't have her like this. He pulled back and pressed her head back on to his chest. She wept, her body shaking so hard.

Then she calmed. "I'm sorry. I'm so messed up. God, I want to die." She started to sob again. "I shouldn't say that to you. Or kiss you. I'm so sorry."

She pulled out of his embrace and turned into one of the four fluffy pillows, crying hard. He let her. He didn't want to make things any worse. He had been a gentleman and any attempt to linger could break his emotional resolve. He closed the door behind him without taking a second look at her.

It was going to be a long day and he wanted to rest a little. If only his eyes would cooperate and close in sleep.

30

Amanda couldn't get over the fact that she tried to kiss CJ and he did the proper thing by rejecting her. Again, she had exposed just how weak and unworthy she was. Nothing she did was right. Why didn't God just take her life? How many times had she come on this same journey, like Nikky had, from Lagos to Abuja, to Port-Harcourt to Kaduna and all over the country, partying and prostituting herself? And yet, God preserved her life. She never even came close to a car accident.

Not only that, God allowed her to get saved by a young believer in the Christian fellowship, brave young first-year student, who looked so young and vulnerable, the way Nikky looked all those years ago when she arrived campus newly. A girl so much like Nikky had walked up to her while she smoked weed under a tree, alone, thinking about how she was going to manipulate her grades so she would not be rusticated. And this young girl had preached the gospel of Jesus Christ to her. The simple message had broken her down, less than four months ago. It couldn't have been anything but God because the first time she attended the fellowship, the girl was shy, even scared to go near her.

She knew God wanted to use her, but she had so much baggage in her life she doubted she'd ever be a true believer, capable of serving God not to talk of leading others to him. Her personal demons continued to haunt her down. The moment she won one battle another pursued her. Why would she start kissing CJ in her moment of pain and grief? She liked him but these were habits of seduction she constantly prayed against in her privacy, and the first moment of weakness, she fell. He wasn't even a believer. How could she ever minister the gospel to him when she had already compromised?

Thoughts of what lay ahead overwhelmed her and she stood in front of the wardrobe CJ stocked with different outfits for her, wondering how she'd face him. It was already noon and she knew they would expect her to join them shortly. She was grateful he bought different outfits because she could never wear the T-shirt and jeans of the previous day again. She picked the only dress in the lot, a simple peasant dress that stopped just above her knee. She wore her slip-on shoes and repacked her hair into a bun at her nape. She walked to the full-length mirror in the room and took several deep breaths, then stepped out of the room.

Emeka sat on the couch he slept on, eating bread and fried eggs. He looked up when she walked in.

"CJ is waiting at the lobby. The DPO wants me for questioning." He drank from a large mug of hot chocolate. "You see now? They want me for question. What am I going to say?"

Amanda's stomach rumbled. "Is there more food?"

Emeka pointed towards the refrigerator. "We put some food away when we came. Warm it in the microwave."

Amanda didn't think she wanted to eat anything from inside the car with the memories of when she entered it last, but her stomach twisted again. She picked a sardine sandwich and a can of coca cola.

"I hate police problem—"

"You have a lawyer with you." She took a seat on the single chair. "CJ will take care of you."

"That's what he said too." Emeka finished his meal and scratched his head. "He said I can confess everything, and he will do plea-bargain for me."

"And he will." The sandwich was surprisingly good. She got another from the fridge. "I mean, if he can get that animal *Kearuruala* out!"

"I believe so." Emeka stood. "We were waiting for you. Be fast, let me finish this questioning and disappear."

"Disappear again." Her eyes widen. "After last time."

He paced. "I still can't believe Nikky never told you where I was all this time."

"Did you want to be found?"

"I wasn't lost. She said she didn't want me to contact you because you would be unhappy I worked for Chief Kalu." He sighed. "That you hated the boss."

"I do. I've had an unpleasant encounter with him before. But she also knew how worried Mama was about you and how that affected me." Amanda finished her food. "She knew I thought you were missing. Or dead."

"Anyway, that is past now. She has died. For no reason." He heaved. "This CJ lawyer, I fear him o. He's like a spirit."

She stopped eating and gazed at him. "What happened?"

"I pretend I'm asleep and he come and lie on the carpet. Two minutes, he's fast asleep, even snoring."

Amanda shook her head. "He doesn't sleep."

"How do you know?" Emeka gasped. "I wait. Even move close to him. I know the police will want to arrest me. That DPO asked how I take know where the accident happen. Anyway, the man is asleep. I open the door quietly. When I get to the lobby, he's standing there by the door. Ask me where I think I'm going if I don't go back up, he will mess me up."

Despite herself, Amanda smiled. "Why would you try to run?"

"Two of us did not sleep after o. He sat there looking at me, asking me every question on earth." His phone rang. "Hello?" He picked up and listened to someone who sounded as though they were wailing.

Amanda walked over to stand beside him, but she couldn't hear anything audible. Emeka exclaimed suddenly and stamped his feet.

Amanda touched his arm. "What is it? Who is it?"

He moved away from her and listened a little more. After a minute or so, he calmed the caller down, mentioning CJ's name more than twice. Then he hung up and turned to Amanda.

"That was Chomi's sister." He groaned and bit his finger.

"Yes?" Amanda turned around to face him. "What did she say?"

"They got the result of the main test." He sighed. "They have to do another operation." He gesticulated with his hands. "She was crying so I no hear her well." He scratched his head. "Chai, that girl just come suffer for this life for no reason."

Amanda sighed. "That's why I never joined in for the ex-rated, animal bullshit!" She cursed. "Regardless of how much they wanted to pay. How's she though?"

"They need another 250k! Or else they can't do the surgery. Say plenty things damage for her body." Emeka cried. "Chomi is going to die! Chai!"

"CJ will pay. We just need to tell him. Now." She headed for the door.

Emeka's eyes widened. "He will pay? Chai! Chai!"

31

— · —

DPO Aliyu remanded Emeka in custody for a day and then released him on bail. CJ agreed to wait just for one more day to be sure he took Emeka back with him to Lagos. In exchange for protection and a light sentence, which CJ assured Emeka could be converted to a fine, and some hard labour without incarceration, Emeka made a full confession of the activities of Chief Kalu in Abuja and Lokoja, to the best of his knowledge.

The pathologist was able to give some preliminary results on the corpse on Wednesday. The most traumatic being that the person had not died immediately. Full results were not due for another two weeks. He also had the coral beads Amanda identified put in a box for further identification. She broke down and wept but each time CJ tried to touch or hold her, she shrank from him as though he was a plague. More than once, he wished he had kissed her as hard as he wanted and apologized later.

After several arrangements were made to move the corpse to Lagos for a decent burial, and the needed two hundred and fifty thousand naira sent to Chomi's sister for her surgery, the group of three flew back to Lagos. They took an Uber to CJ's house for a meeting because he knew going to his office would be disastrous. He'd missed two court sessions and a pile of work awaited him. In over ten years of practice, he had never missed appearing in court, and he knew why now. Amanda had him twisted between her dainty fingers and he couldn't help it.

First, he needed to secure a safe house for Emeka because he didn't trust the gang network Kalu operated would not find him. At last, they decided to keep him in a church's old people's home. After a few calls, he got one and drove Emeka there. Though he hated it, Emeka was glad to have somewhere to lay low until further notice with a room to himself. Amanda warned him not to try and escape because he would definitely fall into mischief.

"I'll tell Mama to bring your favourite oha soup." She teased. "Stay safe."

As they pulled out of the old people's home premises, CJ told her he needed to get to his office. She merely shrugged.

"You can't be angry with me forever. I did the right thing, and you know it," he said.

"I'm not angry with you," she mumbled.

"You won't even let me touch you."

She looked out of the window. "Because I'm not that kind of girl, anymore."

"I know." He sighed. "And I know you were grieving. We all reach out when we grieve." He badly wanted to reach out to her. Somewhere inside, he missed her, whatever there was to miss.

"What's next now? Are you turning me over to the police, too?"

He arched his eyebrows. "Should I?"

She snickered. "Yes, you should. I am wanted. And now Nikky has been found, I have to face her mother."

"Talking about Nikky, you have to stop feeling guilty about her." He slowed down to meet up with the traffic. "If she hadn't found you, she'd have found someone else. You can see she enjoyed the lifestyle."

She turned to him. "It wasn't a cool lifestyle. I knew I was sinking."

He met her gaze. "We all feel like that at some time. There is no true peace anywhere."

"Only in Jesus. I have peace. My life has not changed much outwardly. I struggle with lying. I even tried to kiss a man who didn't want me." She giggled, which turned to a sob. "But I have peace now, deep down. You can have it too." Tears slid down her face.

CJ reached out and cleaned her tears and she didn't flinch as she had done since the day before. "Are you trying to preach to me, young woman?"

She nodded heaving through her tears. "I'm not worthy of it. Any of it. But God had pity on my soul and saved me." She cried. "And I want the whole world to know what he did for me. Because he can do it for anyone. He can do it for you."

He smiled. "Goodness, you have me tearing up, Amanda. Can you stop, I'm driving."

She nodded vigorously and turned away, sobbing and mopping her face, trying hard to control her outburst. CJ had never had anything so touching hit him in the bottom of his stomach. How many times had pastors walked up to him and read him "the act?" Making him realize his soul was lost and he was going to hell with all the criminals he helped walk free? How many times had he gone to bed at night feeling miserable and empty? Asking himself where else and what else could give him joy and peace. He had everything. Money was the least of his problems. He could enter any office, travel to any country, live anywhere he pleased. His job was tough, but he loved it more than life and enjoyed it, but the deep hollow remained like the Grand Canyon, a wonder to him.

He could be with any woman. Except for this one. Sometime between yesterday and today, he'd concluded she didn't want him, and it would be better to go their separate ways when all the Nikky puzzle was solved. No woman had resisted him so persistently. Only Amanda. And it made him want her more. How ironic that she would be the one he wanted and couldn't have. The one whose broken words of condemnation would make more meaning to him than a pastor's oratory.

The traffic moved along and finally in the ensuing silent tension inside his car, they arrived at his office. It was after closing hours and Alice, silly girl, had left. He reckoned she'd been leaving the office at the exact time, a luxury due to his absence. He had Amanda sit inside his office while he printed several documents he'd need for her case. There was no way he was going to let her sleep one night in police custody.

Then he called the DSP and arranged for a meeting at the police station close to her house where she had been locked up initially.

"I can't apologize for preaching to you," Amanda said as they left his office.

He glanced at her. "I don't expect you to."

"I knew I could not reach you, anyway." She twitched. "After my conduct."

"Give yourself a break," he muttered.

"If I'm not locked up, I'd like to go to my mum's house...family house."

They got into his car and he didn't say anything until he was on the way. "You're not going to be locked up. And all you need to do is give me the address of your family house."

"Thank you," she murmured.

32

Amanda stated her name and occupation into a tape recorder, then the detective who had come with Akin to take her, introduced the other people in the room; Barrister CJ, accused's lawyer, Detective Pius and myself, Detective Okoye.

"The accused has agreed to relate all that has transpired in the last month with respect to the disappearance of Ms. Nikky who is her roommate. Over to you."

CJ nodded and she took a deep breath. "The girls came to tell me there was a party in Abuja—"

Pius cut in. "Which girls?"

"You don't have to answer that," CJ said. "Until we determine their relevance to the case." He motioned for her to continue.

Amanda nodded. "I told them I don't do those parties anymore because I had decided to...to change. They laughed and left. Nikky was in the bathroom. When she came out, she asked me who were those, and I told her." She swallowed. "She begged me to give her the details. She said she was broke and needed a party badly."

"Did you think Nikky was broke?" CJ asked.

"No. She had boyfriend…boyfriends, who gave her money."

Pius flashed CJ a warning look. "So, she went to the party you introduced to her?"

"Yes. I told her who to ask for the details of the party. She thanked me and picked her phone to call the person. I didn't get the details of the party because I wasn't interested."

She glanced at CJ who stood across the room, rigid, his arms folded across his chest. The interrogation room was dank and had a dull stink. She knew he couldn't wait to get out. He had tried to make them hold the questioning at his office to no avail.

"What were these parties like?" Pius snarled.

She sat up. "Men, booze and girls. Sometimes drugs."

Pius sneered. "Are you confessing to doing drugs at these parties?"

CJ growled. "Detective, if you don't follow procedure, I'm going to take her away and you'd have to get a warrant to arrest her."

Okoye took a tentative step towards CJ. "We just want to know what she knows about Nikky. For now. Amanda, tell us about Nikky."

Pius swatted the air around him and kissed his teeth.

"Thursday, May 16 was Nikky's birthday. Final exams were to start first week of June. She told me she was spending the evening with her boyfriend. The following day was supposed to be the travel day to Abuja. And she called me when they were leaving." She sighed. "On Sunday morning, I discovered my coral beads were missing when I was preparing to go to church, and I called her to ask about it. She denied taking it. I got upset with her because she takes my things." She looked at CJ who nodded. "My beads are what I used to identify her body." She sniffed. "On Monday her boyfriend came to look for her and I lied she went to class."

Pius growled. "Why did you lie?"

"Because I was trying to protect her relationship. I called her after he left. Her phone rang but she didn't pick up. Tuesday morning, the phone did not go through and I started calling other people I know must have gone to the party. They all said Nikky met a guy who wanted her to stay until Monday, and he would fly her back."

CJ cleared his throat. "Did they give you the name of the guy?"

Amanda shook her head. "They all said they didn't know. He was a random guy who came to the party looking for a girl to take with him for another day."

Okoye paced. "Then what happened?"

"I got worried after six days—"

Pius shouted. "Six days! Your roommate disappears and you do nothing for six days!!!"

Amanda didn't know what to say. CJ had warned her not to answer questions he didn't approve of or blank statements. She looked at him for guidance.

"We're not in a law court. Shouting at my client and trying to intimidate her, adds no value to this meeting, Detective." CJ gestured to Amanda. "Why did you wait for six days before doing anything about your roommate, and what did you do?"

"I had my final exams coming up, so I was a little preoccupied with my studies. Nikky disappears for days sometimes so, six days wasn't unusual but her phone not going through was."

She sighed. "I asked everyone I could without raising any alarm. Besides, I lived this life before. A random guy comes, and we follow. If he pays the right price, we stay. Nikky could have been back in Lagos and with one of her numerous lovers."

CJ urged her on. "So, what changed?"

"Her number wasn't going through and that was strange. And I didn't have any of the contacts of her boyfriends." She dropped her gaze to her hands. "Besides, I wasn't that carefree girl who didn't care anymore. I was trying to live right. Do right."

After a long pause, CJ spoke. "Do you have any other questions for her?"

"Our investigations will continue. She has to return every Tuesday because she's on bail," Okoye said.

"You'll be seeing me, thank you." CJ waved at her to stand. "We can leave."

"Useless prostitute," Pius muttered.

Amanda briskly walked out pretending she didn't hear what the saucy detective said, especially since CJ said nothing too. In the car, she gave him her family house address and again, they drove in complete silence. Her neighbourhood wasn't the nicest, but her mother had refused to leave her father even though he treated her with such disrespect. At least they didn't have a landlord to pay rent to, her mother would say. Even if she and four children shared one room in a house with six bedrooms, she still believed she should stay with her husband and raise her children in an unhealthy, dysfunctional environment.

CJ parked by the road when they arrived. "This it?"

"Yes." She picked her rucksack from the back seat, and another bag her new clothes were in. "Thank you."

"You're welcome."

"Am I supposed to go with you to the station on Tuesday?"

"Nope."

"Why are you quiet?" She couldn't stand it anymore. "Did I do or say something wrong?"

He cocked his head. "Nope."

"Thank you for everything. And for going to Abuja, and Emeka, and all the money you had to spend." She swallowed and unsure of her feeling and why she would, she leaned over and gave him a peck on his cheek.

CJ reacted almost violently and grabbed her head before she could retreat. Panicked and feeling stupid all over again, she bent her head and his kiss landed on the crown of her head.

He pushed her back. "Get out."

She picked her stuff and hurried out. He zoomed off before she had closed the door.

33

—·—

The house was still the same. Amanda knocked several times before Memunat, her step-sister opened the door. The eighteen-year-old girl looked at her for a minute as though she couldn't recognize her, then stepped back. Old feelings of hatred and disgust overwhelmed Amanda. This girl wasn't even her father's child, but she had more power and rights than her mother's children. Her father had married her mother with Memunat's pregnancy from another relationship.

Amanda didn't want to speak to her. It was close to nine o'clock and her father sat in the family room, with her step-mother, both on the couch, their favourite position when in that room. Their five children were sprawled all over as usual and the TV was on to the news channel.

"Good evening, Papa." She bent her head. "Good evening, Mama Ada."

Ada was her name as the first daughter of the family until her father changed it to Chinasa, her second name, because his new wife wanted her daughter to be called Ada. When she got admission into university, she changed it to Amanda.

Mama Ada grunted. "*Ewele.*"

A mixture of old dirt and ammonia filled the room and Amanda left quickly. Mama Ada had a way of saying many things she did not understand or bother to. They were likely her local language, which Amanda had no idea or interest in. She walked to the back of the house to the small room her father confined her mother to. Close to twenty years and her mother continued to suffer. She knocked knowing nobody entered this room except she and her brothers. Her mother would know it was one of her children.

The door opened with a jerk, and Amanda's mother stifled a cry. Amanda hugged her neck, tears clogging her throat. "Mama."

"Ada *nwam*!"

Though there was electricity in the house, the room was lit by a big lantern. After the long minute of emotions, she pulled back. The sweet smell of mint herbs filled the room. Nothing had changed in the last eighteen years. Amanda dropped her bags by the bed, joy unspeakable filling her heart. After she gave her life to God, she had told herself she needed to come back home to her mother. For no other reason but to just be with her. She hadn't been here in close to four years. She looked around the clean and tidy room. The small table with the chair pushed into it, and the small stove on the tables was still the same. The single bed was neatly made. Bags were stacked against the wall and some under the bed, where some pots were also pushed against the wall.

Amanda sat on the edge of the bed. "Do you hear from your boys?"

Mama sighed. "Uzo is still in the village and Gozie is doing his mechanic. Everybody is fine." She slouched. "Will you eat? I have some *fufu* left."

Amanda's lips trembled as she struggled to control her emotions. "And Emeka. Emeka is back in Lagos. I found him, Mama." Tears pooled in her eyes.

"Ehn, Emeka. You found Emeka?"

"I found your baby, Mama. Your favourite boy."

Mama laughed but Amanda saw the tears stream down from her eyes. "I told him you will cook *oha* soup for him and bring."

Mama jumped. "Ehh! *Chim-o*! Thank you, my faithful father, in heaven."

"Calm down, Mama. Before your enemies will complain you're happy and look for small sorrow for you." Amanda laughed. "God is faithful, Mama. Even me, I finished my studies. I finished from university!"

Mama fell on her knees and bowed her head to the ground, then lifted herself and raised her hands up in the air. "You said you will finish. After all these years. You said you will finish."

Amanda's phone rang and she found it in her bag. "Ah, Mama, please let me pick this call. It's my...my friend." She tapped to pick it. "Hello?"

****

CJ breathed hard as he drove out of the neighbourhood and back around the street to the next. He couldn't believe he did that to her. Or she did that to him too. What was going on? Okay, agreed, she was a muddled junk of emotions and couldn't figure herself out, he understood that. His clients, especially the innocent ones, displayed a plethora of behaviours he sometimes hired a counsellor to work with them. Why was he behaving the same? He liked her, a lot, more than was good, more than like, love...she obviously battled the same feelings and emotions. Why was he fighting it as hard as she was? He understood her. He'd tried to date a few "born again" girls in the past. Once he had sex with them, they ran off crying "sin" which he found ridiculous. Amanda was fighting her urges in a unique way, but it gave him no right to shove her or be rude.

He turned his car around and returned to her street. For several seconds, he parked and stared at the house he suspected was hers, an old rickety story building on a street full of its kind. Many girls from this type of area ended up in prostitution and crime, but she had opted to go to school, get a law degree, hopefully make something of herself. He could never agree a girl should mess herself around but at least this one made an effort to break out of the vicious cycle of poverty.

"Hello, I'm outside your house." He licked his lips. How did a voice make so much difference in a person's heart rate?

"Outside, oh my. I...did you forget something?" She seemed to pant.

"I want to apologize for shoving you. Asking you to get out." He breathed through his mouth.

"I'm sorry too. I shouldn't have...have—"

"Can you come outside, or it will be okay to see you tomorrow?"

"I'm with my mum now. Can we do tomorrow?"

"Sure. I can pick you up. To my office?"

"No. I'll find my way. Thank you." She paused. "Please send the address."

"I will." He rubbed his forehead. "Do you accept my apology?" No woman had ever made him feel so frustrated, or annoyed, or depressed, or in need.

"Only if you accept mine."

"I do." He sighed. He wanted so badly to see her. "Thank you. Tomorrow then?"

"Tomorrow," she said quietly. "Thank you. Goodnight."

She hung up before he could say more. Well, this was better. He had to let her know how he felt. Make it official, ask her out. It scared him more than facing Chief Kalu on the opposite side of the law.

34

—·—

With the pile of work waiting for him, Thursday morning was crazy, but CJ couldn't help checking the time every half hour. At lunch break, he fought the urge to call Amanda. When did she plan to show up? At first, he was anxious, and then he became angry. Wasn't it just pure courtesy to let him know she wasn't going to show up? Unable to bear the waiting any longer at two, he called her number. It rang out.

Alice walked into his office as he started to redial.

He arched an eyebrow. "What?"

"Amanda is here to see you."

He lost his voice for a second and cleared his throat. "Ask her in."

It took another several minutes before she walked in wearing a simple floral dress and black pumps.

"Good afternoon," she said.

He waved her to a seat, and she took it, wondering why his heart would not slow down. She looked so beautiful in the dress, but he couldn't form any words. How on earth did she succeed in getting him so jittery?

"I'm sorry I didn't come in the morning. I went to pack my things at my house."

"Oh, yeah." He put down his phone and took his seat behind his desk. "How did it go?"

She heaved a heavy sigh. "You won't believe it. Alaba was nowhere in sight. The door was broken down, house vandalized."

"What?" He exclaimed. "And your stuff?"

"I got some, but a lot was burnt. Nikky's things too." She shook her head. "Very sad."

"Do you know who?"

She shrugged. "Slopo, maybe. Or some other campus boys. Akin too."

"Sorry about your things. It hadn't occurred to me to get your place secured." He arched his eyebrows. "What are your next plans?"

"I hope to find a job. After all of these cases are cleared."

He leaned forward and then remembered she seemed to have a magnet on him and rested back. "In the short term?"

"Help my mother with what she does." She looked down at her fingers. "I've not been there for her in a long time."

"What does she do?"

"Oh, she sells wares. Makes little things, food, snacks, hair, mends torn clothes, even knits." She snickers. "She's your perfect jack of all trade."

"How about coming here to work for me?"

She gasped. "Work for you? As what?"

"Are you not a law graduate? You can start an internship until you go to law school." He waved towards his door. "Just like what Alice is doing."

She followed the gesture of his hand. "What about her?"

He scoffed. "She's tired of me already but she has several months left to work. But I can have you too. And I pay well." He half-smiled. "I'll even get you a new wardrobe."

She covered her mouth with her hand. "Thank you. Oh, my goodness. I've been praying to get a job to help finance my law school." Tears pooled in her eyes. "Oh, thank you so much."

He bit on his lower lip. "My pleasure."

She clasped her hands. "I won't need a new wardrobe. You've done more than enough already. And I still have many of my clothes. Thank you."

"Campus clothing." He opened his phone. "You can contact this woman and discuss with her. Most of the ladies in the office wear her label."

He handed the phone to her and studied her as she copied the number. When she was done, she returned his phone.

He kept it aside. "Can you start now? I got a call from Chief Kalu. There is a lot to do on that case right now."

Her beautiful eyes widened. "Yes, I can. Thank you."

"Sure." He stood, feeling tight and dry in his throat. "Excuse me." He walked to his fridge and brought out a canned juice. "Have you had lunch?"

"Yes, thank you."

He returned to his seat. "Do you punctuate your every word with thank you?"

"You've stunned me with your kindness." She paused. "I never thought I'd get a job like this. So soon."

"Speak with the fashion woman today. You'd have to get your hair done as well. There is a look I expect in my office." He turned to his laptop. "You'll work eight to five Monday to Friday. Some Saturdays too if there's a reason. Before you leave today, I'll have HR know you're coming on board. Do you have a resume?"

"Yes. Yes, sir. But I don't have it here."

He looked at her. "Sir? How inappropriate!"

She smiled and dropped her gaze to her hands. "You're my boss now."

He took a long sip from his juice. How was this going to work? Seeing her every day, wanting her every minute? The thought of employing her had come to him the previous night as he turned and tossed and searched for the words to win her heart. It was brilliant. He wasn't going to ask her out for a date and face rejection, he was going to see her every day of the week, and some Saturdays, every Saturday if he had a say about that, and he would be attending her church very soon, though she didn't know that yet. Just that he hadn't envisaged seeing her and not being able to touch or love her would cause so much pain. Could he do it? He wasn't an easy person to work with. Perhaps some of her bad traits would come off seeing and working with her and his infatuation would fade.

"Come with your resume tomorrow. When is law school starting?"

"November, I think, but I can't meet up with this year anymore. Because of the results."

"We'll see," he mumbled. He made a note to place a call to the school and see what they had to do to get her in. "We'll need to get you a laptop but for now, you'll do without."

She nodded. "Okay."

"Chief Kalu has been briefed by his men in the force and he wants me to represent him. If it gets to that." He tapped on his laptop. "Listen to this."

It was a recorded call. He made it a habit to record all calls that came into his phone, especially job-related. Even his clients knew his calls were recorded. While the conversation played, he studied her and beat himself mentally for asking her to work for him. She'd be a huge distraction. She gasped and moaned in response to the discussion and the sounds sent chills to his loins.

"Excuse me."

He walked to the connecting office to inform Alice Amanda was joining the team and to allow himself to breathe normally.

35

—·—

E meka stared at Amanda. "See how you're fine, Chinasa. This CJ has turned you into a queen."

Amanda giggled. "That's the only thing you've been saying since we walked in."

Mama smiled. "He did not even look at his mother two times."

"Don't mind him. After you made that sweet soup for him upon all he did." Amanda rolled her eyes. "Mama you haven't seen in four years."

Emeka laughed. "I should not show appreciation for my fine sister?"

"Anyway, apart from bringing Mama to see you, some things came up and I wanted to discuss with you." Amanda sat on the double bed in Emeka's room. "Hope you're okay here?"

Emeka shrugged. "I'll live. The old people don't worry me. What came up?"

"Chief Kalu called CJ. He's in Lagos and wants CJ to represent him. He was arrested in Abuja and released on bail."

Emeka jumped from the side of the bed where he lounged, startling Amanda and Mama, who sat on the only chair in the room. "Aruruala is here?"

"Calm down." Amanda exhaled. "First, this place is safe. No one knows you're here except us and CJ. And no one knows we know, and we will keep it that way."

Emeka stole a glance at Mama's furrowed face. "What of you and Mama?"

Mama clasped her hands. "Nothing will happen to me. Is two of you I worry."

"And there's nothing to worry about." Amanda smiled. "CJ is preparing a very strong case. I just need you to know this is serious and Emeka, you need to lay low. Here. Don't go drinking or doing anything stupid."

Mama frowned. "He should come to the house with me?"

"No. He's okay here. Chief Kalu is looking for you, Emeka. He doesn't know where you are now, Abuja or elsewhere so he's looking," Amanda said. "But he has boys in Lagos, so you need to be careful. Especially because he also knows you helped us escape." She sighed. "The good thing is that he doesn't know the identity of the people you helped to escape. CJ says he's priming him and will be watching both of us."

Mama gripped her chest. "So, coming here now? The man will know?"

"It's possible. But I don't think anybody followed us here. We just have to be careful."

Emeka dropped his head into his hands. "Aruruala is here in Lagos!" He raised it sharply. "So, CJ is his lawyer?"

Amanda shook her head. "CJ is your lawyer. That's why Chief Kalu is uncomfortable."

The conversation with Emeka got heated after Amanda tried to make him realize he was safe. Her brother raised all the reasons why it was better for him to leave town if the evil kingpin was around. In the end, she had to leave him with a stern warning to remain until he got a go-ahead from CJ. She had a headache by the time she left, and a worried mother to calm on her hands.

Papa sat with his wife and five children in the parlour, watching the evening news as he did daily. Knowing he never responded to their greetings was not a reason to leave it out, so Amanda bent, as did her mother, greeted and escaped into the back corner of the house where an old store had been converted to a room for Mama. She hated being here, but she had only started working for CJ three days before. What she had saved as a student could get her a one-room studio apartment but she wanted something bigger so her mother could at least have a room to herself. Seeing the way they were treated though, she had second thoughts. Maybe it was better to move out, first. And then make better plans later.

Amanda dropped her bag on the bed and took her shoes off. Mama sat on the bed and pulled her to sit too.

"Is Emeka going to be alright?"

"Yes, Mama." Amanda nodded. "CJ also has some people watching him as he is in that place. Though he said I shouldn't tell anybody."

Mama heaved a heavy sigh. "Ah, because I am so afraid. As two of you argue about the chief."

"You have nothing to fear, Mama." She smiled. "We have everything under control. These three days I worked with CJ has been so educative. The guy is good."

"Hmm." Mama pressed her lips together. "So, when am I going to meet CJ? Because since you enter this house, it is CJ this, CJ that. If not he is your boss, I will say you want to marry him."

Amanda laughed, her voice a tone too loud. "No o. Nothing like that. He's my boss." She stood and started to undress. "He was even in church today. I was surprised. I would have introduced you to him."

Mama clapped. "I will still meet him one day one day."

"Heh, Mama! Okay, you will meet him."

"He goes to your church?"

"I just saw him today." She wore her nightgown. It wasn't late enough to sleep but the room was usually stuffy. "I didn't even know he took note of the name of the church when I told him."

"Maybe he wants to know if you're lying about going to church," Mama smirked. "Some men are like that o. They want to know everything."

Amanda shrugged. "Maybe."

But she knew CJ had come to the church because of her. What she wasn't sure of was if he had been genuine in going forward to the altar when the pastor called for people who wanted to surrender their lives to God. She had battled with that. He hadn't even seen her at the time. It was after service closed she hurried to say "hello" and that was it. He didn't say anything to her. He was an extremely intelligent person and she wrestled with the feeling he was trying to play mind games on her just to get her in his bed. Well, if he was genuine, he would never ask for intimacy with her, which somehow saddened her. Their relationship now was boss/staff and he had maintained a professional profile. Several times in the last few days she had struggled not to show how attracted she was to him. Especially with the lousy Alice who didn't seem to have a lot of decorum.

Mama moaned. "Hmmm, CJ every day. We shall see."

Amanda giggled again despite herself. "So, Mama, I want to even discuss this house thing with you. Me, I can't stay here again, and I won't leave you here. With these horrible people. In this small hole." She climbed on the bed. "They don't care for you. And all your children have left home. We were the reason you decided to stay, not so?"

Mama sighed. "Na so, my daughter. But after Emeka left, there was nowhere for me to go."

"Well, there is where to go now. I will get one room for us. After, I can get two rooms."

"What will we need two rooms for? Will that not be too costly?" Mama swatted the air in the room. "Did I not live inside here with four children?"

"And must you suffer forever?" Amanda smirked. "Mama, we'll get a good place and you too can start to live for once."

"Thank you, my dear."

"I need to sleep now, Mama. I have to be out of the house very early in the morning."

Mama smiled. "To go to the CJ office."

36

Team meetings held every day for thirty minutes besides Monday morning when they had an extensive one. In all of the two and a half weeks Amanda had worked with CJ, he never got to the office later than any of his staff. His conduct was professional and though she noticed he sometimes stared, there were no inappropriate gestures toward her. He attended her church the following Sunday from the first time, and then the following Sunday but never made a mention of it. She had quickly aligned herself as well, making sure she kept her feelings in check. Whatever he had felt must have been infatuation and she had to fight hers as well and deal with it.

As was her custom, she made sure she arrived as soon as she could and living far helped. She woke up early and got into a bus before the morning rush and usually got to the office before the others. She'd say a short prayer at her desk, and then pop into his office to register her presence. He never gave her any assignments or discussed with her unless there was a job he wanted her to do, and this would only come up after the morning huddle, as they referred to the morning meetings.

She knocked on his door and entered after his prompt. "Good morning, sir."

He stood beside his desk. "Good morning. Two things. Your brother left last night and is not back to the old people's home."

Amanda gasped. "What?"

"My guy said he went to a club." He arched an eyebrow. "I'm going to lock him up when he gets back."

Amanda exhaled visibly relieved. At least, someone knew where he went. "He deserves it."

"Chief Kalu has been trying to get the best legal team as things heat up so we can't become careless." He shoved his hands in his pocket. "Also, the pathologist called last night. Nikky is coming in today."

Amanda clasped her hand over her mouth. The feelings of guilt had almost disappeared as her life seemed to have stabilized in the last two weeks. Though they were actively working on the case, she was lost on the initial emotions.

"Once the body arrives, I'll want us to go and meet it together. And then we accompany it to her village." CJ touched a piece of paper on his desk, while she continued to take in the news, trembling.

"Yes, sir," she mumbled.

"You may want to read this, the autopsy report. So you have the full details." He handed her a few sheets. "Nikky didn't die immediately, apparently."

"Her mother will be devastated," Amanda whispered.

"She is likely going to file a civil suit against you. A guy contacted me, said he was her lawyer and wanted us to discuss the next course of action." He stared at her. "I don't think they have a case. But I'm gathering my own evidence."

"Yes, sir."

"You'll notice on that report, they did not identify the corpse."

Amanda frowned. "Why?"

"Nothing to compare the DNA with. The pathologist's office have no access to Nikky's dental records or DNA or her parents'." He sighed. "I wrote her mother since we returned requesting for a sample to be sent to the pathologist but got no response."

"I'm not sure her mother will willingly give any but I know. That was Nikky."

"If you have any additional information you want to share that'll help a civil case against you, send an email." He shrugged. "Otherwise, I don't think they have any case."

She shook her head. "I don't have any information other than what I gave you already. About Nikky. And me."

"No problem." He took his seat. "I won't be at the huddle. Nikky is coming around noon, and I want to be ready."

She nodded, unable to find the words beyond the heaviness in her throat.

He turned his attention to his laptop. "You may go. I'll let you know when we're ready to leave."

Amanda returned to her office on wobbly feet. She shared the space with three others; Alice, Jude, an office assistant, and Billy, an investigator. Six lawyers worked on CJ's team and they shared two other offices. She wasn't sure she could face anyone at the moment, but CJ had not mentioned she could take any time off and she didn't want to ask for unnecessary favours. She could bury her head in her laptop and pretend to be busy. Well, not pretend actually. She had work to do, and she was still searching for a house, and there was the pathologist's report CJ had printed out for her. She wondered why he didn't just send the soft copy to her. She closed her eyes and took deep breaths to calm herself. She had to read it up, there was no avoiding that. Better she did before she faced Nikky's family. She checked her watch and the next person who normally came into the office would not arrive for another twenty minutes. She opened her eyes and read the summary.

Nikky died between twenty-four and thirty-six hours after the accident, in which she was flung out of the jeep. Suspected cause of death was internal bleeding. Amanda gagged. If Emeka's tales was anywhere close to the truth, they could have saved Nikky's life when they went to retrieve the jeep and Austin's body. Only if they had searched for the others in the vehicle.

37

A van with soldiers drove in front of the hearse bearing Nikky's coffin, a military police officer drove CJ's car with him and Amanda seated in the back, behind the hearse and another van with soldiers drove behind them. At the sound of the siren, people came out of their houses, most wearing white garments that flowed beyond their ankles.

CJ glanced at Amanda. "Are you alright?"

She nodded but he saw tears slide down her cheeks beneath the dark glasses he had gotten for both of them. She hadn't needed any persuasion to put it on. He reached out before he could stop himself and cleaned the tears with his bare fingers. That throbbing in his heart and groin he'd become so familiar with started again. Amanda kept her hands clasped in her laps, but the flow of tears increased. He pulled out a handkerchief from his pocket and pushed it into her hand. She blew her nose into it.

A massive church building loomed ahead. CJ had never seen anything like it. More people wearing white garments trooped in as the military van pulled up in front of the church. A group of singers all in white stood in a circle at the side of the huge blue and white building, singing. A woman in the middle flung something that looked like a vial, sending off strong incense into the air. Billy, his investigator, had liaised with the family and the church for the funeral arrangements, and ridden in the hearse. He got down and walked over to CJ's side.

CJ wound down his window.

"They're not taking the coffin inside," Billy said. "There's a short service, and then to the burial ground. I think her father's compound is where they're burying her."

CJ twitched. "What are we to do now? Go in the church?"

"No, we can't. As you can see." Billy looked around. "It will be an exclusive service. But we can join them for the interment."

"Okay. Let's know when they are done. You'll lead the way."

"Sure."

"Thanks," CJ mumbled. He turned to Amanda. "We'll wait until the end of the service."

Three hours later, the worshippers trooped out of the church and walked away down the street. CJ couldn't help but wonder where Nikky's mother and brother were. The hearse turned on the sirens again and they drove slowly down the street from the church to a side street where many people were gathered in front of a big compound. They made way for the military van and the hearse but lined up in front of CJ's car. The soldiers in the van behind came out. CJ saw Billy also walk back from the within the compound. He went straight to CJ.

"What's going on?" CJ asked.

"I don't know yet. Seems they don't want too many vehicles. I'll check." Billy walked back towards the group barricading the gate and started to speak to one of them. Four soldiers stood with him. CJ took off his dark glasses and noticed Amanda had leaned forward.

"They will lynch us if we don't leave here." Amanda trembled. "Let's leave. We have delivered Nikky to them."

"You think so?"

She nodded. She took her phone out of her purse. "I changed my number but Akin got it. Sent me this text a week ago threatening me." She showed him.

"It doesn't say anything about the funeral, just that he'll deal with you." He squeezed her hand. "Don't panic."

Someone knocked on the window beside CJ. They both looked up to see Billy.

"We have to leave. The soldiers in the other van will sort themselves out," he said. "I'm coming with you."

CJ motioned to his driver. "Open the front for him."

The driver did and Billy entered. "They say there's an ambush for us. The other van will lead the way."

CJ saw the other van reversing, almost hitting the troop of worshippers loitering. They succeeded in clearing out of the street but didn't join a main road.

Billy turned partially. "The other driver said he'll not take the way we came. He knows these areas very well."

"Okay."

CJ had hardly finished talking when something like a stone hit the windscreen. The glass cracked. CJ yelled and at the same time pushed Amanda. "Get down."

More stones hit and smashed the windows. They heard a gunshot. And then another. CJ and Amanda remained crouched in the floor of the back seat. The car entered a rough terrain but kept moving. CJ had his hand on the back of Amanda's neck, and kept it there. For several minutes they seemed to be driving through an uncharted road, then Billy spoke.

"We're clear. Wow. Mad people."

CJ raised his head. "Stay down until I tell you to get up," he murmured. Amanda whimpered a response.

He lifted himself on to his seat and surveyed the environment. They were on a narrow dusty road in the middle of the forest, but he could see the two military vans flanked them front and back.

"I have a complete record of this attack, CJ." Billy lifted his phone. "This is complete rubbish."

The driver grunted. "These village people. That's how they do. If you didn't come with us, you'll be dead."

Billy cursed. "They don't fear soldier?"

"They don't care," the driver said.

CJ shook his head. "You didn't get down when I told you to?"

Billy smirked. "How will we get evidence."

"You can't risk your life like that!" CJ tapped Amanda. "We're safe now."

She lifted herself slowly and sat, her hands and lips trembling uncontrollably. He pulled her into his arms and patted her back as she sobbed.

"They said the hearse driver too ran with us," Billy said. "One of the soldiers just sent me the message. So, we're all out of there. We'll arrange for the vehicle to be removed later."

CJ leaned back and closed his eyes. "Thanks. If they like they should leave their coffin in the vehicle."

He had spent a fortune in the past month on this Nikky's case and knew he had more to spend. Yet, this was what he got? The most important thing though was that they were all safe. Akin had written his office through a lawyer they were pressing criminal and civil charges against Amanda. He wondered what they would have to say when he exposed the type of woman Nikky was, and how she had gambled her life up until this brutal end.

Amanda's phone started ringing and she checked for the caller. "It's Akin!"

"Pick it. Put it on speaker. Everyone quiet." CJ took out his phone and started to record video.

Amanda did as he said. "Hello? Akin?"

Akin growled. "If I don't finish you next time call me a bastard!"

"What did I do to you?" Amanda sobbed. "It's not my fault Nikky decided to—"

"Shut up your mouth!" He yelled. "Shut the *eff* up, you *bee*!"

CJ jolted as he tried to stop himself from interrupting.

Amanda panted. "I have not done any wrong. And you should face that."

"Come back again, whether you will not be more rotten than Nikky's corpse by the time we're done with you." Akin's voice broke. "You wicked soul. After all the way we supported you."

"You never supported me. I fought my own battles!" Amanda cried. "You knew how I survived. You and your mother!" Akin yelled something but Amanda continued to scream. "And you knew how Nikky survived."

"Nikky did not need to survive! We gave her everything. We paid her school fees and her upkeep, rent, transport! You spoiled her!" He screeched. "You spoiled her and killed her."

Amanda's shoulders shook as her pain overtook her and she wailed. CJ took the phone from her hand and hung up. He stopped the recording and pulled her into his arms.

"They opened the coffin?" Billy gasped. "Disgusting people."

38

CJ gave her the rest of the week off and Amanda chose to use the time to intensify her house search. She had gotten a couple of options and wanted to check it out with her mother. Tuesday was difficult for her as Akin kept calling and sending threatening messages. She reported all to CJ who advised her to get another phone and switch this off. She bought a new phone and told her mother it would be hers until her "broken" phone was fixed. Mama was grateful for the new gift.

They met a realtor at a two-room studio apartment in Surulere. It was a bit pricey and the woman, likely in her thirties, wanted rent for one year and agency fee for three years. The location was beautiful though and the neighbourhood clean and serene. Another option was closer to her office in Ikeja, a one-room studio with kitchen and sit-out. It was less expensive, but the landlord wanted two years rent advance.

"What do you think, Mama? I'm thinking we can ask them to allow us to cover the sit-out, it turns into a room. And we'll have two rooms." Amanda and Mama stood outside with the realtor. "It makes more sense for the price."

The realtor shrugged. "I can talk to the landlord. If you'll do a neat job. Usually, he will agree but you'll have to take it down when you're leaving."

"I won't have a problem with that." Amanda shrugged. "Mama, what do you think?"

"I like this one as it close to your office. But the other one better, but cost."

Amanda laughed. "You have done nothing to help this decision, Mama."

The realtor smiled. "If you ask me, take the other one. By the time you partition this one and paint, the money you will spend will be more than the other one."

Amanda snorted. "But you want three years' agency fee! What if I don't stay there for up to three years."

"It is refundable," the woman said.

"I'll give you a call. But we definitely need to move in. If possible, this week."

The woman gasped. "This week? I hope I can see the landlord to finalize. I'll call him but make up your mind on time."

Amanda nodded and shook her hand. She called an Uber and they returned to her father's house.

"We need to start packing. I'm going to call the agent and collect the Surulere one." She scratched her neck. "I will ask for a loan from the office to make up what I have."

"They will give?"

"Ah, they will give o. Because we need to move from this place. It's even too far for me to work." She took her shoes off. "Do we even need all these things in the house. We should just pack our clothes, Mama."

Mama clasped her hands. "Anything you say."

For one emotional moment, Amanda felt sorry for her mother. No woman deserved to be treated with as much disdain and disrespect as her mother had suffered in her marriage. It had been believed at the beginning that Mama Ada used diabolic powers to assert herself, but did those things work for so long?

She took the new phone from her bag and started to send a text message to the realtor. A loud bang of a door stopped her. It was quickly followed by two gunshots. Without thinking, she grabbed Mama and they ducked behind the bed. Thanks to her tidy mother who had very little in the way of personal items, there was enough space for two, not much for hiding, though. Amanda closed her eyes and clenched her teeth. Akin's threats rang in her mind. She should have known he would find her here. How, she didn't know, and didn't care. More gunshots and slamming of doors rent the air. Heavy footsteps climbed the staircase over their room and returned down. Mama Ada screaming and her children, and more gunshots. Then there was total silence.

Tears slid down Amanda's face as she continued to control her emotions. Her mouth filled with it, and her heart. What just happened? Who was hurt? Why would Akin do this to her family? She hadn't done anything to deserve this height of wickedness. Mama remained dead still, and Amanda stayed frozen beside her, unsure of what to do. Time passed and then she heard a loud scream and wailing, then voices.

She pushed away and whispered. "Mama, stay here, please."

Mama accepted with a nod, and Amanda tip-toed to the door. It seemed several people were moving up and down, in and out of the house. The back room they were in was under the staircase and anyone would easily pass it off for storage. Her sweaty hand clutched the new phone and she leaped into action.

She called CJ, and tearfully related what happened. He told her to stay exactly where she was until he arrived. Then she finished sending the text message to the realtor.

"Can we move in tonight?"

39

Everyone seemed to be outside when CJ drove up to the street that led to Amanda's father's house. He found a parking space ahead and walked back with Billy, and one of the other lawyers, Ehis. A woman sat on the floor just outside the door, flanked by two other women, all wailing. People loitered, some with their hands raised to their heads, others speaking in hushed tones. A police car was parked with the lights silently flashing. CJ walked to the car. There was no one there. Nobody paid attention to them, so he walked into the house.

A uniformed policeman took pictures of the bloodiest scene CJ had ever seen and doesn't acknowledge their presence. A thick smell of blood mixed with human faeces filled the room. CJ counted three dead bodies scattered across the room. Billy started to take pictures too. CJ and Ehis stepped out immediately. CJ called a police emergency number and then Amanda.

"I'm outside," he said softly. "Tell me what part of the house you're in and I'll come and get you."

Two minutes later, Ehis and CJ knocked and opened the door to the small room under the staircase, the back room, Amanda had called it. There was no space for both men to enter, so Ehis stood at the entrance. CJ had to bend to enter. Amanda rushed into his arms, weeping. He hugged her tight.

She cried. "I don't know why Akin will come here and shoot. Did anyone die? Did he kill anybody?"

"We saw three bodies in the parlour. We will stay here until the policemen I called arrived." He stole a glance at the woman who sat on the floor with her face buried in her hands. "Is she alright?"

Amanda hiccupped. "Yes, my mother."

CJ leaned over. "Mama, good evening. I am CJ, Amanda's boss. And this is Ehis, one of our lawyers."

Mama raised her tear-streaked face. "Ah, *Oga* CJ, see how we come meet."

"You'll be alright, Mama. Don't worry." CJ sat Amanda down. "Can you tell me what happened?"

"We went to check a house. Came back at about seven." Amanda stuttered. "It's not even ten minutes. I was about to send a text message to the agent that we wanted the house. We heard a loud banging, someone slammed the door, then two shots." She swallowed. "Then more noise, screaming, shouts, more shots and all went quiet." She looked at him. "We ran behind the bed and stayed there until there was no sound again, then we came out and I called you."

CJ nodded. "We just need you to leave here safe, first. We'll go to the police station to give a statement. Then we can find a hotel for you and Mama."

"Yes, sir. Thank you."

CJ checked his watch. It was close to midnight. The room they were in couldn't take one more adult and at his height of over six feet, he couldn't stand straight. Why would Amanda's mother agree to live here like a house rat? It made no sense. Ehis leaned against the wall, his face flushed with a mixture of emotions. CJ wanted to pace but there wasn't enough room for it, so he squatted beside Amanda and checked his watch every five minutes.

His phone rang later, longer than he wanted, and he described where he was in the house. Two uniformed policemen knocked but could not enter and stayed at the entrance.

The first introduced both of them. "I'm Sgt. Ilori and this is Detective Ambode. We have a vehicle outside, and the emergency management people are taking the bodies." He glanced down the corridor. "Is there a back door? We don't want to tamper with the work going on in front."

Amanda breathed heavily. "There's kitchen door, which leads out."

"Good. Lead the way. We are parked a little up the road. Outside is bustling with activity," Ilori said.

"Thank you for not taking them through to see the mess in the parlour," CJ murmured.

Ilori led them to his vehicle but CJ insisted Amanda and Mama ride with him. Billy met them up front and they all left the scene of the killings.

"I spoke with one or two people outside, who live close to the house," Billy reported. "It's gang-related."

"Gang?" Amanda gasped. "What kind of gang?"

Billy shrugged. "No one knows yet. But the neighbours are cooperating with the police. The CSP sent at least ten men. They are all there."

CJ stole a quick glance at Amanda who sat beside him in front. "Body count?"

"Four. Not yet identified."

She covered her face and wept into it. CJ badly wanted to comfort her but in truth, he'd had a hard time in the past few weeks keeping his hands off her, and with the emotions she'd displayed over Nikky's arrival and the trauma they experienced in the village, he feared he would disgrace himself if he let his emotions down any further.

They rode in silence to the station where Amanda gave a statement and then CJ dropped Ehis and Billy off at their homes. He drove to an exclusive guest house buried in a clean neighbourhood close to his office, already occupied by Emeka, and put them in a room.

Mama and Amanda hugged him tightly.

"I was so worried about you with Nikky's burial and all, I didn't remember to call you," Amanda said. "How are you?"

"He's safe. And so are you. I own this place and I use it for my witness protection," CJ said. "You'll be here until we crack this case at least."

Mama bent in the manner of respecting elders in their culture and thanked him. CJ left them, fagged out. He was back in his house before he remembered Amanda had mentioned getting some accommodation. He made a note to ask her to put it on hold.

40

— • —

Though CJ called to find out about their welfare daily, Amanda wanted to get back to work and be free to move around. As soon as there was a little break in the senseless attack on her family, which took the lives of her father and three half-siblings, she pleaded to return to work. He declined. The investigation was able to exclude Akin from the crime but hadn't placed it on anyone else. One of the killers was associated with an area gang it was proven Nikky's people had no contact with. The guy was in hiding but CJ was sure he would soon be found.

Meanwhile, they now had two separate cases linked with Nikky. Her mother's lawyer had fixed a meeting, and Chief Kalu also got a lawyer to contact CJ. Amanda suspected a third case would also come off from her father's murder. And there was Slopo, who was out on bail but steaming and doubtless would seek revenge for his damaged leg.

Amanda walked into the office a little earlier than usual on the first day after her one-week leave was over. CJ had told her to stay away until he thought it safe enough for her to start work again, but she couldn't. As expected, he was in his office, brows furrowed, gaze focused on the open screen in front of him. He looked up when she walked in and stood.

"You shouldn't be here."

She sighed. "I know."

"Why are you?"

She closed the door behind her and took a few steps inside. She hadn't seen him since Tuesday evening, almost a week, and it seemed as though her life no longer existed. What could she say was the reason she came? He kept her updated on the cases, so that couldn't be the reason. The hideout was comfortable, to say the least, and she had her mother and brother close, so she didn't lack good company or food. It was him. She missed him.

He moved out from behind his desk. "Yes?"

Her gaze met his and something shifted inside her. He continued towards her until he was just a breath away. They could be touching but they were not.

"I'm so afraid," she whispered.

He came even closer, his face barely an inch from hers. "You have nothing to fear. The evil will pass."

She nodded and looked down at her feet because if she raised her head her lips would be on his. His heady scent made her feel weak in her knees. She wanted so much to hold and be held, but she knew it wasn't right. His hand touched her hip lightly and she willed her feet to move away but they didn't. A second hand rested on the other side of her waist, she took a deep breath in.

"I missed you," he whispered into the middle of her bent head. "Goodness, I think I have tried my possible best to stay away, and you come here. Tempting hell out of me, looking so beautiful."

She couldn't help herself, she fought hard to not lean into him, and she had to breathe through her mouth.

"I don't know how I never noticed you when I was with Nikky, but Amanda, you have changed my life." His mouth started to trace a path over her hairline. "Do you feel what I feel? Do you think there's a future for us?"

Her gaze shot up to meet his. He lowered his mouth to hers, but she turned. Just in time. Her heart raced faster than she thought was good.

He stepped away suddenly. "You know what? I don't even care what you feel." He walked to his desk and opened a drawer. He returned to her and backed her against the wall.

She licked her lips. "CJ."

"Don't say anything. I want you." He searched out her face. "I don't claim it was instant, but you've grown on me." He placed kisses on her eyebrows. "You preached to me, and though I called your bluff, I got back home, and cried like a baby. I wanted God, and I wanted you. Still want both." He rolled his nose over her face. "I'm not fighting it anymore, Amanda. I don't care what you think of me, or how you feel. I'm not fighting loving you anymore."

A cry escaped her lips. "CJ."

He slipped on to both knees and opened the small box in his hand. Amanda stared at a gold engagement ring, the diamond stone glimmered. She clasped her hands over her mouth.

"Will you marry me, Amanda? I swear, I have never given anyone a ring and I'm thirty-four. I love you. I really love you!" He gazed up at her. "Please."

Tears gathered in her eyes. She swallowed hard. He wanted her to say "yes" wanted her to respond one way or the other, but nothing came from her throat. She gripped his head and drew him up with so much energy, she thought she'd snap his neck. Her mouth met and clung to his fiercely, and he kissed her back.

She tore her mouth away, remembering her vow not to kiss until after marriage. Ashamed she couldn't even keep that vow. Thrice broken now, with this same man.

He traced kisses over her eyes and neck. "Is that a yes?"

"Yes." She moaned. "Yes, marry me."

They laughed. He slipped the ring on to her fourth finger. It fitted. "Perfect," she cooed.

He cupped her face. "You won't let me touch you until we're married, correct?"

"Yes."

"So, we need to get married this weekend, right?"

"This weekend?" She gasped. "How?"

"How do you imagine I can cope without you in my bed?"

"For someone who just emotionally said they want God, I suspect you." She giggled. "We'll take it one day at a time, darling."

"Ah, darling. You called me darling. That's music in my ears."

Someone knocked and they startled apart but not far enough. Alice walked in and stared at both of them.

"It's time for the team huddle," she said.

CJ arched an eyebrow. "Be right there."

She stepped out, leaving the door ajar. Amanda rolled her eyes, unable to stop smiling despite Alice's rude tone. CJ waited until Alice left before he gave her a quick peck and returned to his desk. "Time for work, babe."

41

—·—

Despite himself, CJ let Amanda come to work every day. He wanted to see her. It wasn't safe to have her leave the hideout regularly in case someone was watching her, but he couldn't wait each day until night so he let her come, and though they both maintained a high professional profile, in spite of Alice's snooping, he indulged a few minutes on a constant basis to be alone with her.

They could not have a normal relationship until there was a definite direction in the mystery surrounding Nikky's disappearance and death. But CJ put himself out there like he had never done before. When he gave Amanda the recovered credit card he had at one time given Nikky, she declined.

"I have over a million-naira-credit limit on that card," he said.

She rolled her eyes. "When it's ten million, talk to me."

"Really?" He snickered. "I have one with ten million."

She pressed her lips together. "A hundred then. I'm not cheap."

To his surprise, she didn't want to take anything from him either, giving the excuse she had nowhere to go to wearing expensive jewellery and that her ring she feared to wear so her finger would not be chopped off. Everything about her flattered him. How could a girl so decent end up with the lifestyle she had on campus? It made him realize how badly an abused child she must have been.

A little crack to the murder case came when one of the raiders on Amanda's home was caught. The eighteen-year-old boy, found by Billy in a drunken stupor, spending some of the money he got from the "job" had driven the getaway vehicle. Under torture, he confessed Chief Kalu was behind the raid. His body was found hanging from the ceiling in the police cell the following day. It was all CJ needed to bring a close to that case from his office. He turned in all the evidence to the office of the prosecutor.

"I don't know why Kalu would order a massacre of your family, but if I regret anything, it's getting him off nine years ago," CJ said after work when he visited with Amanda and her family. "But he's not getting away this time."

They sat in the small parlour attached to their three rooms, after dinner.

Amanda sighed. "It's not your fault. You were doing your job."

CJ leaned forward. "Where's your step-mother now? I never thought to ask."

"At her mother's house." Emeka snickered. "Her evil mother."

CJ arched an eyebrow. "How do you know that?"

"You think I will sit here and be eating and growing fat when my mother and sister are in danger?" Emeka shook his head. "Kalu was my boss."

CJ snarled. "Talk to me, Emeka. What have you been doing?"

Mama clasped her hand in her characteristic manner. "I try to tell him not to go anywhere."

"I cannot sit here, waiting for him to find us, so I enter town."

"And what did you find?"

"Aha, Barrister CJ, must I tell you? Have you not made progress?"

Amanda gasped. "You found the boy who was killed. Isn't that too risky for you? Chief Kalu is still looking for you!"

CJ frowned. "Could he have been looking for Emeka when he went to your father's house? And in anger killed everything he saw?"

Emeka took a sip of the juice he'd ordered since Amanda disallowed any alcohol. "He knows I will not go to my father's house."

Amanda shivered. "Me. He must have gone to look for me."

"He doesn't know you. He went to look for my mother." Emeka sighed. "Kearuruala does not bear his name for nothing."

Mama's mouth dropped open. "Me? Why?"

"To torture you." Emeka shrugged. "That's what I was told. He figured if he killed everybody except my mother and one or two siblings, that will make my mother miserable forever and I will come after him in anger. That way, I will come out of hiding and he can destroy me." Emeka hissed. "Maybe even torture me and my mother first."

"I have wondered why he did not kill everybody." CJ exhaled. "That's his style, isn't it? You go after him, and he makes a mess of you."

"He thought Mama Ada is our mother," Amanda said softly. "What a brute to plot such evil."

Mama wrapped her arms around her waist and exclaimed. "Eh!"

"I want to assure you of your safety." CJ held Amanda's gaze. "He'll soon find out he got the wrong mother, that's if he hasn't already. But he will never come near here. I have some military men checked in to other rooms. No stranger can storm here and get away."

"Thank you," she whispered.

CJ stood. "I have to leave now. Emeka, please be responsible. I'm counting on you to take care of your mother."

Emeka nodded. "Yes, Barrister."

"If you hear or see anything. No matter how stupid, let me know." He held out his hand to Amanda. She took it. "Good night, Mama. I'll see you tomorrow."

Mama moaned. "Goodnight, my son. May God be with you."

42

— · —

CJ wanted them to sit in his car and talk. Then he had Amanda sit sideways in the driver's seat, and he sat on the floor kit, literally between her legs.

He held her hand. "I can't sleep until all of this is out of the way. I can't bear the thought that that monster was so close to you the other night." He kissed her palm.

She played idly with his scalp. "He made a mistake coming after Emeka in such a brutal way. He'll soon get caught."

"I regret ever defending him." He cackled. "What goes around comes around, isn't it?"

"Don't talk like that. I'm sure there are quite a few who are truly innocent."

CJ bent his head and letting go of her hand, covered his face with both of his. "I wish that could be true." He swore. "I feel so rotten."

Amanda leaned over and placed her chin on the crown of his head. "Why did you choose to defend criminals? Is it for the money?"

He smirked. "When I was fifteen, I had sex with this thirteen-year-old girl in the neighbourhood. I mean, we were sort of dating." He sighed. "Well, it was in her house and somehow her parents got to know and filed charges against me that I raped her."

"Goodness."

"My dad was angry and initially refused to do anything about it. He was a high court judge at the time. Mum ran around and finally got me off the hook without jail time." He snickered. "Paid a huge fine. Dad got involved then, but I was so upset about the whole thing. I told myself I would defend people whether they were guilty or not." He looked up at her. "I'll kill myself if Kalu touches you."

"He won't. I may be anything, but I take care of myself. And God has been on my side for a while." She smiled. "I'll kill myself if you kill yourself."

He chuckled. "Romeo and Juliet." He stared into her eyes. "No kissing, you said?"

"Hmm mmm."

What she saw in his eyes scared her. It mirrored what was in her heart too. A yearning too deep to comprehend.

"I love you, Amanda."

She closed her eyes. "I love you more." She breathed in. "So much more."

"Let's get married. Tomorrow."

Her eyes flipped open. "CJ! It's not possible."

"It is. We'll leave town for a few days. Go to a registry somewhere obtuse like, Ota or Ibadan."

Her laughter interrupted his plan. "Obtuse! Ibadan is not!"

"Okay. Remote. Like, huh, Ikire. Or Epe. Their registries won't be busy. We can just walk in and marry."

She bent backward and continued to laugh.

"It's not funny, Amanda. It is possible. People in developed countries do every day."

"And what happens to all the cases on our necks? Kalu, Akin, Nikky?"

He dropped his head back to lay on her knee. "Nikky is not on my neck. Kalu will soon be caught and I'm defending Emeka against him. Akin. Who's he?"

They both burst into laughter.

****

CJ insisted Amanda stay away from the office though he missed her so badly, he decided it was safer to keep her out of view. Kalu could get to know she was Emeka's sister and may go after her. The tragedy he meted out on Mama Ada and her children left him cold. But for the meeting with Akin, he wanted her around, so he went to pick her himself a few days later for the scheduled occasion.

A group of six people led by their family lawyer, Barrister Ilupo, arrived in CJ's conference room, where he insisted he wanted the meeting held. All wore the long white gowns, except the lawyer. CJ had them sit on one side of his long table, while he and his team – Amanda, and Billy, sat on the other side. Ilupo had been in court with CJ only once, a man who boasted of over thirty years on the bar. CJ had dismembered his case into silly bits and from the way the old man glared at him, this looked more like a personal payback than anything else.

Ilupo cleared his throat. "Shall we proceed?"

"Sure." CJ arched an eyebrow. "What's your case?"

He had read the brief and shared it with Amanda and Billy, but it still needed to be read out. Ilupo adjusted his pair of glasses and read from the pages of the document before him. Nikky's family held Amanda, Emeka and their mother liable for Nikky's death and were going to file a civil suit.

"Demanding a total of eight point five million naira from these three evil persons." Ilupo wet his fingers with his saliva and removed the piece of paper which he set aside. "We will submit this after we leave here, Barrister CJ. Over to you."

"Thank you, Barrister Ilupo." CJ tapped on his open laptop. Billy and Amanda did the same. "Can you acknowledge you got my email and response?"

"I did," Ilupo said.

Nikky's mother stood and began to pace along with three women with her. Akin leaned over and said something to Ilupo. They had a hushed conversation then he sat back and fixed his gaze on Amanda.

"You know I am representing Amanda, Emeka and their mother in this suit of yours and I have asked you to provide reasonable evidence against them. Do you have that?"

"This girl," Nikky's mother pointed at Amanda. "Took my daughter and turned her into a—a what she's not supposed to be. With her brother, they pimped her and made money off her. Until they drove her to her death. May God's thunder fire you!"

CJ frowned. "Can you calm her down, Barrister Ilupo?"

"Your children and your children's children will never know peace!" Nikky's mother yelled at him. "The same way you are defending evil people, evil will visit you!"

"It's his life. He looks at guilty people and helps them walk free!" Akin snarled. "And you will cry. This time around. You messed with the wrong people."

The three women started to jump and chant at the top of their voices. "Fire! Eli! Fire! Eli!"

Amanda caught his attention with a little tap of her pen beside his laptop. "CJ?"

"We'll wait it out," he muttered.

One of the women started to spin really fast. "You need to stop this, Barrister Ilupo," CJ said. "Or you might get a different case."

Ilupo exhaled. "Can you excuse us for a few minutes?"

CJ stood with the other two and left the conference room with their devices. Outside, he chuckled. "Ilupo is going to regret ever taking this case. Eight point five million, my foot."

43

—·—

Barrister Ilupo had his team under control an hour later when he invited CJ back inside. The three women were seated on the floor in a corner, quiet. Nikky's mother and Akin flanked Ilupo.

"I told you I have evidence of Amanda encouraging Nikky to go to the parties, thus pushing her to her destruction. And I have witnesses who will happily corroborate this." Ilupo pushed a list across to CJ. "This is a closed case. My clients are also ready and willing to negotiate with you. Nobody wants to drag this longer than necessary."

"Oh, Nikky!" Her mother burst into tears. "I will fight until your killers are brought to justice."

"It's okay, madam," Ilupo said stiffly.

CJ glanced at the list and passed it on to Amanda, who read through a little longer and then passed it to Billy. Billy kept the list and typed furiously into his laptop.

Akin snapped. "We will accept five million. That to you is just a chicken change. The kind of money you drop for prostitutes like her to lie down for you." He tossed his head in Amanda's direction.

"We haven't started to negotiate, Mr. Akin." Ilupo moaned. "They want to confirm the names on the list first."

"Not quite," CJ said. "I have evidence to counter whatever you have and whoever is on that list, is probably on my list as well."

"What do you mean by that?" Akin slammed the table. "What does he mean, Barrister?"

Ilupo scratched his head. "He will let us know in a moment. Just calm down."

"I have them all resolved, CJ." Billy looked up from his computer. "I sent you the link."

"Thanks, Billy." CJ pointed to the multi-media screen in the room. "The people on your list."

Everyone turned their attention to the video that came up. Billy closed the blinds and the room went dim. Two boys showed up on the video, Slopo, and another. Though the volume was up, they said nothing. Both rolled up marijuana and began to smoke.

CJ murmured. "Taju Ahmed, a.k.a Slopo. Nikky's boyfriend and the other person is not a student. His name is Christopher Adu. Supplies weed to the students most of the time."

Nikky came on the screen and greeted the boys. They roll up weed for her.

Her mother screeched. "This is not my daughter! God forbid. God forbid!"

Slopo drew Nikky into him and kissed her on the mouth. The three women jumped to their feet and this time had incense which they began to sprinkle as they shouted, "Eli, Jehu! Eli, Jehu."

CJ pretended he was unaware and continued to watch the video, his brows drawn tightly. The scene changed to that of Nikky with five other girls in a room. They did drugs and lay stoned.

"Ronnie, ring-leader of the girls, Amanda, Tope, Gina, Vic. All these girls except Amanda are on your list. This video doesn't say much. Until you see this." CJ growled. "Amanda asking Nikky to leave with her."

In the video, the girls all lay stoned. Slopo walked in with two men.

CJ muttered, "Slopo and his boys. Terry and Ajayi."

They tapped the girls. Amanda sat up and looked for Nikky. She dragged her up and would have left with her. Nikky snatched her hand away. Amanda left alone. The three men started to have an orgy with the five girls.

Akin shot to his feet. "God punish you for showing this nonsense. Stop it!" He screamed. "Stop it!"

Nikky's mother dropped her head on the table, and banging it, wept. Tears streamed down Amanda's face and she pressed her lips tightly to keep from making a sound.

CJ powered off the projector and Billy turned on the light. "I have six more videos. Apparently, Nikky loved shooting videos. Sex with animals, with multiple men, with girls half her age." He glared at Akin. "With her big brother!"

"I will deal with you." Akin stomped off shouting. "Fire burn you!"

The three women stopped their drama and hurried after him. Nikky's mother stood, and for a moment CJ could only feel pity for her.

"May the devil eat your soul." She spat. "The seven curses of the devil follow you all the days of your life." She stomped out after her people.

Amanda stammered. "I reject all of it in Jesus' name. Amen. You're blessed beyond any curse."

Ilupo stood. "You knew this will come down like this, didn't you?"

"I warned you, Barrister. Some of her friends were looking for her to retrieve these videos. She used it to blackmail even her friends." CJ shook his head. "To think I thought I was in love with her. I thought I would marry her."

"You?" Ilupo laughed for the first time. "You were bewitched too. I bet she had videos of two of you."

"If she did, it's just sex between a man and a woman," CJ muttered.

Ilupo grunted. "How did she shoot videos like that, when she's in it?"

CJ motioned to Amanda to answer. "She did selfies sometimes, or she'd set a timer and place it somewhere. She was really good with that," Amanda said softly. "I found the hard drive where she saved the videos when I looked through her things for clues for where she was."

CJ moaned. "Awful."

"What a child. When you told me the videos were bad, I didn't believe you." Ilupo carried his file and bag.

CJ arched an eyebrow. "So, are you going ahead with the civil suit?"

"I have no intention of continuing with the damaging evidence you have. If her family wants to continue with the civil suit, I wish them luck." He snapped. "I know if you were their lawyer you will continue and cheat your way to a win for obvious criminality."

CJ stretched his hand for a shake. "Every man has a right to legal representation and deserve the best of our efforts. It's the oath we swore."

Ilupo eyed the stretched hand with a frown. "Good day, Mr. CJ." He stomped out.

CJ rubbed his hands together. "I just need a few minutes alone."

Billy left but Amanda stayed.

"He had no right to judge you," Amanda said.

"I'd seen those videos but seeing them with her family." CJ swallowed hard. "It's tough."

"Nikky played too hard." Amanda sniffed. "I didn't understand it most times. But I couldn't warn her. She'd shut me down, tell me I was worse and I taught her all she knew."

"She bit more than she could chew." CJ clenched his jaw. "Thanks for giving me the videos, darling."

She nodded. "I know I was close. I did a lot of what she did too. But after God saved me—" she broke down and wept.

"You can't blame yourself for her lifestyle."

Amanda dragged in a shuddering breath. "There's something I want to tell you and I'm so afraid...but you need to know."

"Tell me."

She straightened her shoulders. "I have told myself it may lead to the end of our relationship and I will not blame you if you choose that."

CJ smirked. "You said you didn't have sex with an animal."

She sobbed. "I didn't."

He breathed through his mouth. "Then what?"

"When I was seventeen, I had an abortion. It wasn't properly done." She bit her lower lip and was quiet for a long time. "For a few days, I just kept pumping myself with antibiotics to kill the pain and infections. Nothing changed. Bleeding was worse." She looked at him, her eyes filled with tears. "They took the whole thing out." She wailed.

CJ frowned. "The whole thing? What?"

"My—" She swallowed. Her gaze went to her stomach and back to his face.

"Your womb?"

She nodded. "Yes."

CJ swung out of his seat, breathing hard. "Why? Dammit!" He closed his laptop with a slam, took it with him and marched out of the conference room, Amanda's cries trailing him.

44

— . —

C J returned almost immediately and dropped his laptop on the table. Amanda's heart thudded. She'd thought she'd have a few minutes to mourn before she quietly left. She couldn't blame him. She would leave such a person too if in his shoes. He drew her up and hugged her, and her tears overwhelmed her all over again.

"I'm sorry." She sobbed. "It was just the first time, and I vowed I would never abort another baby if I ever got pregnant. I just got sicker and it was either take it out or I die. I'm sorry."

"Ssh. Ssh." He pressed her head into his shoulder. "It's okay."

"I have dreams. I see my baby every time." She sniffed. "I will tell every girl on earth an abortion is not worth it a bit. I am sorry. I am so sorry."

"I'm sorry I walked out on you. It's not like I'm a saint." He cupped her face. "Look at me. I'm sorry, too. I'm sorry I have to marry a woman without a womb!"

She gasped and looked at him, but he was smiling through his tears. "Oh CJ, I love you so much. Thank you for accepting me."

"So, this is the plan." He sniffed. "I need to have kids. I must."

"I was looking through the internet about options. And we can get a surrogate. They will use your—your seed with her egg—"

"Hell no. If you can't have kids, then I can't too."

"CJ?"

"Yes. The first two years of our marriage, no kids. I want to enjoy my wife." He kissed her forehead. "Then we start to adopt. I want four at least."

Amanda drew his head down and clasped her mouth over his. She pressed her body into him, provoking both of them. When they came up for air, CJ exclaimed.

"What kind of woman are you? I thought you said no kissing."

She hugged him tightly. "I'm so weak. Will I even make a responsible wife?"

"I think you'll make a great wife and mother. A lawmaker, though, I don't think so. You'd make and break your own laws."

She laughed into his chest. "I think you're right. We should get married. As soon as possible. Even the Bible says if a man cannot hold himself, he should marry."

"But I can hold myself. I do until you drag me down with you."

She looked up at him. "Well, he who finds a wife finds a good thing. So, let's do it."

He sat and put her with him on his lap. "Here's the deal. My parents are very scrutinizing, and they will want to know everything about you. So, it's good I asked one of my friends in Law School to see how we can get you enrolled this year."

"What? Oh, thank you! That's if I graduate."

He shrugged. "You will graduate, and if you don't, then we'll say you're in your final year." He chuckled. "And remember not to mention it's your third year doing finals."

She played with his thin moustache. "I thought you didn't want to marry a student. Nikky said you didn't."

"I guess I didn't want to marry Nikky. Thank God, I didn't. But you, young woman, are a different ball—"

Alice walked in and folded her hands across her chest, her face scrunched disapprovingly. "Mr. Yemi is on the line for you, CJ. He said he's been calling your cell, no answer."

CJ arched his eyebrows. "You can see I'm busy."

"Busy!" Alice laughed. "CJ, he said it's serious."

Amanda stood. "You should take the call, I guess. And I need to tidy up my report on this morning's meeting." She blew him a kiss and turned to pick her laptop.

He picked his. "Okay, darling." He walked out.

Alice's eyes widened. "You're sleeping with CJ?"

"Of course not!" Amanda sneered. "We're engaged. When I told you I got engaged? That's him. Now, I really need to finish my report."

Alice blocked her exit. "Are you joking? When? How?"

"Alice! We're still at work!"

"At work! And you're sitting on the boss's laps." Alice cried. "You know, I've been here longer than you and CJ is a bull to work with. Since you joined us, though, hmm, now I know."

Amanda laughed. "Well, you know better. We don't bring the relationship to work."

"Huh!" Alice screamed. "So, if you bring it to work." She gesticulated. "You'll be going naked in front of all of us."

Amanda rolled her eyes. "Alice, may I go?"

"CJ has changed. I'm not kidding you. I've been wondering. Hmm, how did get him?"

CJ stood at the door. "Alice, please excuse us."

Alice left with a smirk on her face and CJ entered.

"Did you speak with Mr. Yemi?" Amanda asked.

"Kemi, his wife, is packing. He wants me to come and see if I can beg her." CJ shook his head. "I've been warning him. You don't mess around with a wife like Kemi."

"Wow. Sorry to hear that. I'll Uber back to the guest house."

"Can you come with me?" CJ sighed. "Yemi was weeping on the phone."

45

Yemi ran to meet them in the driveway, his clothes drenched. "We've been at it since morning. The children didn't go to school."

CJ gasped. "Calm down. What happened?"

Yemi glanced at Amanda. "Thanks for coming too."

Amanda nodded.

"What happened?" CJ repeated himself.

"She saw a message on my phone. Said I was cheating." He threw his hands up. "That's it. After all I've done for her. She said she's leaving me and taking the kids."

Amanda heaved. "Where is she?"

"I'm not cheating. Heaven knows the girl has not even agreed for me." Yemi sighed. "Just one message from the useless girl."

"Take us to where she is, Yemi." CJ snapped. "And will you calm down?"

The scene at Yemi's house was a mess. Kemi had packed three suitcases and was packing another in the boys' room. Amanda had never seen anything so gross since her father threw her mother out seventeen years ago. Two boys, between the ages four and ten stood in the corner of the room, weeping.

Amanda noticed they stood separately side by side and not hugging or touching. Seeing those boys brought tears to her eyes. It reminded her so much of she and Emeka, terrified beyond reason as their late father and Mama Ada flung bags out the door, and their mother wept and begged. When her father finally agreed, they were given the space under the staircase.

Amanda hurried to the younger boy and carried him and drew the older one under her arm. Kemi noticed for a moment she had company.

"If you like bring the Queen of Norway, Yemi. I'm tired and I'm done." She stuffed boys' clothes into a full suitcase. "Please, who are you? Why are you holding my boys?" She glanced at CJ. "CJ, please leave."

Amanda couldn't control her tears. Her emotions rose to the fore and with how the day had started, seeing those videos with Nikky's mother, her breakdown and fear after confessing to CJ, and now this.

"Please, Aunty," she sobbed. "Please, don't go, please." She fell on her knees.

Kemi paused. "Who is this, Yemi?"

"My fiancée, Amanda," CJ said. "Please, Kemi will you let us talk—"

"Amanda?" Kemi glared at Yemi. "Is she the one? Amanda, CJ's babe!" Kemi lunged towards Amanda and tried to snatch her sons from her.

Yemi hurried forward to hold her but she flung her fist at him and caught his left eye. CJ held her by the waist.

"Kemi, will you stop this? Amanda means no harm!" CJ shouted. "Please, for God's sake, calm down."

"Yemi has been having an affair with your girlfriend. And he has the audacity to bring her to my house!" Kemi screamed. "Let go of my boys before I break your head."

Amanda cried harder and held on to the boys.

CJ frowned. "What do you mean?"

"Tell your friend what you have been doing with his babe." Kemi freed herself from CJ and returned to trying to zip up the full suitcase. "I'm done. There's even nothing any of you can do or say."

CJ faced his friend. "Yemi? Talk now before I kill you."

"I just used Amanda's name to save the number." Yemi rubbed his left eye where the punch landed. "I'm sorry. I thought it was smart to hide it that way."

Amanda closed her eyes briefly. She really couldn't imagine anyone lie with her identity like that.

CJ pushed Yemi. "Yemi! Are you mad? Are you crazy? Why will you do that? Why—"

"CJ, please, can you take him outside? Please," Amanda murmured.

With the men outside, Amanda raised herself up and sat on the bed, still holding both boys. She stared at Kemi, tears still streaming down her face.

"He saved her name as Amanda, CJ's babe." Kemi shook her head. "How can he do that?"

Amanda sniffed. "One moment there, I was so afraid he would deny and say I'm the one. CJ would never take me back. Not after Nikky's senseless cheating."

"I'm sorry I shouted at you. But you should leave. CJ is close to our family and I would have loved to meet you under normal circumstances." Kemi swallowed. "You shouldn't see me like this."

Kemi held her forehead. Amanda could imagine the kind of headache she'd have. She studied the beautiful woman Yemi was married to and wondered why men cheat. CJ had told her Yemi's wife was a medical doctor who managed her own family planning clinic, and the two had been in love since high school. Her long permed hair was a mess and drenched in sweat, her peasant dress too. She looked more than a couple sizes bigger than Amanda's eight, but no one would call her fat.

"You are my big sister. That's how I see you." Amanda rocked the younger boy and noticed the older one no longer cried. "And CJ has told me so much about you. I want to be your small sister."

Kemi smirked. "Well, too late."

"Is there anything you can look at and just give your relationship a second chance?" Amanda sniffed. "Because CJ and I don't plan to let you go."

"Can you imagine Yemi calling everybody on the phone and telling then I want to leave him?" Kemi mopped sweat off her face with her dress. "People have been calling my phone all morning. He called my parents who don't live in Lagos!"

"He doesn't want you to go. He was crying on the phone when he called CJ."

Kemi rolled her eyes. "Gimmick." She sat on the bed and her smaller son crawled into her lap. The older went to sit close to her. "If not for these boys, I would have left him since. But I'm tired."

"Can I beg you?"

"No, Amanda. No. Look at CJ, as unmarried as he is, he is never unfaithful to whoever he's with." Kemi swatted the air in front of her. "Is that not a man?"

"Your boys need you and their daddy. I grew up messed up because my parents didn't stay together, in the real sense." Amanda sighed. "I know—"

"Thank you. I'm taking my boys with me and Yemi knows he can't stop me. And my baby girl doesn't need a cheating father. My boys may not have their father in the house but at least, they won't be seeing me looking like this mad woman I am."

Maybe her own words drove deeply into her, Amanda couldn't tell but Kemi bent her head and sobbed.

Amanda shifted to her and hugged her and the boys and cried with her.

46

—·—

Amanda cooked rice and made stew, which the family ate. It was close to ten and no one had had anything all day. After a solemn dinner, Kemi went to bed with the boys. CJ and Amanda sat on the couch in the parlour while Yemi paced.

CJ snapped after all was quiet. "You try this nonsense again, Yemi, heaven knows, I will buy tickets myself and drive them to the airport."

Yemi took a deep breath. "I want to thank you guys. If not for you."

"Just shut up!"

Amanda smiled. "At least, everything is settled. Thank God they didn't leave."

"Amanda, I really must thank you," Yemi said. "You made her change her mind."

"I didn't even do anything. God touched her."

"And I thought you were just one of those campus babes, so shallow."

CJ snorted. "You'd better get your act together. And delete the number you saved under my wife's name!"

Amanda laughed. "Chai, I have suffered."

"Babe, thanks. You really got it together. And after such a long day." CJ squeezed her hand. "Are you good?"

She leaned her head on his shoulder. "Hmm, mmm."

"Great. I guess we should leave now." He looked at Yemi. "You better get your life straight." He stood, lifting Amanda up with him. "I have to be in court tomorrow and I've not done any work today, thanks to you, Casanova!"

"I'll check on Aunty Kemi tomorrow. She said she'll likely be at home all day," Amanda said.

CJ arched an eyebrow. "You can have my car."

"I don't drive, haha. I'll just Uber. Don't worry about me."

CJ moaned. "Ugh, you need to learn, babe!"

"I can pick and drop you," Yemi offered.

"Thanks, but no thanks!" CJ growled.

Yemi and Amanda laughed.

"I think you got it right, CJ. I'm so happy for you," Yemi said. "Amanda is the best one by a million yards."

"Thanks. Good night." CJ led Amanda to the door. "She'll probably head my family law department."

Amanda giggled. "I don't think so."

Yemi saw them to the door. "I want to check on Kemi. If she's still awake, I want to talk with her."

"Just apologize. No matter what she says. You are in the wrong," Amanda said.

Yemi nodded. "I know. Thanks a lot."

"Wow, I have never been involved in a couple's fight like that before." Amanda sighed as CJ pulled away and joined the night traffic. "Wow."

"I'm serious about what I said. Having a family law practice."

Amanda scoffed. "What happens to your defense practice?"

"Not going anywhere but you did a great job tonight," CJ said. "I couldn't fathom how to handle Kemi. Never seen her that mad, and I've known them both for over ten years."

"I was just crying." She giggled. "Couldn't put my emotions in check. Is that what you want for your family lawyer? A crying lawyer."

"It worked. As long as we win the case."

"Hahaha! Soon it will be fake. Everyone will know the crying lawyer who uses tears to win cases." Amanda rolled her eyes. "Not me. No way."

"So, what will you do for me? Besides making me work less and live life more?"

Amanda drawled. "As a lawyer or a wife?"

CJ groaned. "Don't try me."

"Okay, I'll decide for you, since you can't." She rested her head and closed her eyes. "What I want most in life now. Is to be your wife. Will you marry me?"

****

"Can you believe I've known you for just three months?"

"Three months? It feels like forever."

"Is that a good forever or a bad forever?"

"A roller-coaster forever. My life has never been on such a spin. Gosh!"

Amanda laughed. "Because your life had been super boring and work-crazy."

"I'll take work-crazy."

"Over me? Work-crazy over...over—"

"Over?"

"Exciting, fulfilling, enjoyable—"

"Kissing-less—"

Amanda's laughter interrupted him. "That will soon change." She lay flat on her back on the carpeted floor in his parlour right beside the couch where he was on, and stared at the ceiling. "Ten more days! Can't believe I'm getting married."

CJ rolled to his side and stared at her. "Believe it, sweetheart."

Amanda lifted herself on to her elbows. "Your mum, she was talking about having baby showers a month after our wedding."

CJ snorted. "I warned her no babies until after two years."

"Did you hint her the babies will come without us being pregnant?"

CJ dragged in a long breath. "Why would I try that? Are you calling for a third world war?"

Amanda narrowed her eyes. "You know what you say when you are desperate for a kiss." She stood. "I am not falling into your trap today."

He pulled her back on to the couch. "You'll beg."

"Don't try me." She giggled and freed herself. "I have a four o'clock appointment." She called over her shoulder and walked into his kitchen.

He followed her. "With who?"

"Event planner. We're seeing the cake today."

He leaned against the door frame. "Cake will be ready?"

She opened the pots. Got a plate. "Well, the first six. The other eight will be done two days before."

He chuckled. "We're getting fourteen cakes. Are you kidding?"

She shrugged. "Chetamandaweds. It's supposed to be a secret from you. But you make me tell all my secrets."

He walked over and cuddled her from the back. "That is so sweet. I will still be surprised."

She put some pepper soup on her plate. "I'll just hurry over this and take Uber."

"Uber uber. I should fight those people. They make you less dependent on me. And lazy about learning to drive." He pressed a kiss on her neck. "Don't imagine—"

"Wait, my phone is ringing." She wriggled out of his hold and took her phone out of her jean pocket. "It's Emeka. Maybe he's found a house. I told him to...hello?"

"Chinasa? Hello. Is CJ with you?"

"Yes, he's here. Are you okay?"

Emeka seemed to pant. "I have Aruruala. Here. With me."

Amanda screeched. "What?!"

CJ took the phone from her. "Emeka, what?"

"Aruruala! I trace him. I have him here."

"Where? I'm coming over!"

Emeka called out an address and started to repeat himself. "I got it," CJ said. "Just hold him, I'll be there in thirty minutes." He hung up. "Lock the house when you leave for your appointment." He marched to the parlour to get his key.

She dropped the plate and followed. "I'm coming with you."

He stopped abruptly and bumped into her. "No, you're not. First, it may be dangerous. Two, you have somewhere else to go."

"Please, I'll call and cancel the cake-sighting."

He brushed past her, took his key and headed for the door. "Cake-sighting...no. Amanda, no."

"Yes, baby. Please." She stopped short. "Or don't go."

He turned to her. "Let's go. I'm not going to have you crying over this."

She giggled. "Funny."

47

On their way, CJ called for police back-up and Billy. They found Emeka with bruises all over his face and arms, seated beside Chief Kalu on a dirty floor inside an abandoned building. The crime lord was bruised as well and tied to a huge stone that looked as though it was moved there. One young man lay unconscious several feet away. Amanda hurried to squat beside Emeka and fussed over him. The police took Chief Kalu away and asked CJ to bring Emeka as soon as the latter got treated and could answer questions.

"You need an ambulance." CJ took one look at Emeka. "And a job as my investigator. You'll be trained of course."

"You were not meant to take matters into your hands," Amanda cried. "What if he killed you?"

"Amanda is right," CJ murmured and looked at Billy. "Please, get an ambulance."

"I got one already. On the way," Billy said.

Amanda snickered. "Yeah, right. One second ago, you were praising him and offering him a job."

CJ chuckled. "You can't blame me. He's strong and he gets his job done."

She threw her hands up in surrender. "You're impossible. Emeka, where's Mama?"

Emeka leaned back, his face squeezed in pain. "Guesthouse."

She smoothed back his brother locks. "How did you find him, Emeka, this is so dangerous!"

"I sent a message through the vines that my mother wanted to see him. Fool agreed to meet." Emeka breathed hard. "I can't talk, please." He slumped.

"Emeka!" Amanda quickly checked his pulse. "Oh, my goodness. Will he be okay?"

CJ bent over her. "Looks like he just passed out. He should be fine." He walked to the unconscious fellow. "This one seems alive, too," he said. "I'll have to ask the police to come back for him."

The ambulance arrived in good time and Emeka was taken to the hospital. CJ checked his watch and it was just a few minutes to four.

"That cleared up pretty fast." He winked. "Do you want me to go cake-sighting with you, babe?"

Amanda shook her head. "No, and yes. I don't mind the free ride. But I do mind you seeing the cake before d-day."

"I'll wait in the car. Anything to serve you, my love."

****

D-day was a beautiful Saturday morning late August. Amanda wore a simple ivory a-line neck court train tulle wedding dress with beading sequins. CJ wore a crisp white shirt with a black suit and a navy-themed tie. She walked down the aisle alone, struggling not to cry. There had been the option of one of her brothers walking her in, but she refused, to honour the memory of her father, who though was never there for her. The church was packed full, mainly by members of CJ's rich and influential family. Her family, seated just on two rows, gave her hope and comfort she was in the right place. God had fixed her into a family, she who once was so solitary.

The pastor gave a moving sermon about the goodness of God to man and admonished the new couple to reflect the grace of God in the way they dealt with each other. Then he did the joining and they proceeded to sign the marriage register, after which he presented them to the congregation and asked CJ to kiss his bride.

CJ murmured before taking Amanda's lips. "Legal first." Then he fastened his lips on hers.

The excited congregation screamed and cheered. Amanda smiled and hid her face in his shoulder.

"We will now take the thanksgiving offering," the pastor said.

He motioned to the ushers who brought two brass plates and handed them to CJ and Amanda. The lead singer in the band raised a fast song and the congregation was assisted by the ushers to file out in a decent manner. Many had the first opportunity to speak and congratulate the couple and after dropping their offering envelopes in the plates, did so.

On the last row, the last person, unlike the others, wearing a black dress with a black veil covering her face, walked up to the couple and unveiled herself. Amanda weakened and would have slumped if CJ didn't grab her side just in time.

Nikky dropped an envelope in Amanda's plate. "You couldn't wait for me to be gone. Amanda, my friend. I'm back to take my man." She blew a subtle kiss at CJ. "My lover."

CJ clenched his teeth. "You're dead."

It all ended in a matter of seconds. Nikky held her veil in one hand and a clutch purse in the other, snickered and walked back the way she came. If anyone in the church recognized her, they didn't show it. Amanda's gaze followed her.

CJ nudged her and she turned to him. He smiled at her, his eyes expressing his heart, his love for her. "She can't touch us. I'm no longer her lover."

"I know, my only love," she whispered. "I know." She breathed in and smiled for her crowd as the pastor closed the service. "The drama hasn't ended, though."

CJ laughed quietly. "I knew I was in for a roller-coaster when I decided to marry you."

Nikky could be back but she was dead.

48

— · —

Amanda walked into the four-bedroom duplex that would be her new home with CJ following behind and exclaimed. "CJ!"

She turned into his arms and pressed her lips on his. He took over the kiss, but she tore her lips away before it progressed. She wanted to look at her new home. A wedding gift from her husband, all in her name. With a two-bed two-bath visitor's lodge her mother and Emeka moved into two weeks earlier as they proceeded to Ghana for their honeymoon.

"It is so beautiful. The purple and lilac are awesome. My favourite colours." She dragged in a deep breath and ran into the large kitchen.

CJ followed her slowly. "Wait until you see the master bedroom. Designed for action."

"You've had non-stop action in the last fourteen days. Don't you rest?"

CJ laughed. "Action can never finish, my dear."

She opened a big pot on the cooker. "Ahh! Egusi soup? Who cooked?"

He stood behind her and wrapped his arms around her waist. "I told Mum to cook something."

Amanda twisted to face him and dropped a peck on his lips. "She knows my favourite soup. Yours too." She giggled. "Let's eat. I'm just suddenly famished."

"Great timing then because she didn't know if we'd be back early."

"My mother is like that. Very intuitive."

"Thank God for a flight that was on time."

Amanda found a cooler with wraps of fufu and served the food on two plates. "When we finish eating, I'll go and thank her."

CJ chuckled. "Such hunger. I thought you'd thank her, unpack, make love, take a bath, before you eat."

"Make love, that must be on the list, CJ!" She swallowed the first morsel. "Not the way my stomach is screaming."

They settled at the dining and she ate with her hand, wondering why she just got hungry so unexpectedly. Then she drank some water she found in the fridge and sat staring into space.

"What?" CJ arched an eyebrow. "You look sick."

"I feel sick."

She hardly made it to the guest toilet to empty her food, still warm the way she ate it. CJ rushed after her and held her as some of the soup slipped out from her nose.

"I think it's food poisoning." She burst into tears. "The juice I took on the plane."

"Maybe you need to lie down and allow your stomach to rest." CJ led her to the master bedroom.

Despite her sickness, she gasped. "It's so beautiful. The bed is so big."

"Since you like rolling." CJ chuckled. "And throwing your body on someone on the bed."

She smiled. "I feel sleepy."

The sheets were cool beneath her. The last she remembered was CJ taking her shoes off.

Amanda woke up later and found CJ on the other side of the bed, on his laptop.

He smiled at her. "My mum calls this kind of sleep chicken sleep."

"Did I sleep for long?"

"Approximately fifteen minutes." He closed his laptop. "Did you dream about me?"

"No. The sleep was too short, I guess."

"Hungry? I ordered some relatively easy food for home delivery. Chicken and chips."

"Not hungry at all. I might as well have not puked." She stretched. "I feel fine now."

He leaned back. "Good. You scared me. I've never seen you sick."

"I never get sick. A headache once in a blue moon but nothing more." She yawned. "I scared myself."

"Not since seeing Nikky at our wedding have I been that scared."

She laughed. "Nikky Nikky. Die hardest. She stopped sending me messages on social media last week."

"That's because I blocked her from all our accounts. And her name is on a police list of stalkers."

Amanda rolled on to her belly, seeming to find the posture so relaxing. "I don't miss her. One day, we will find out the mystery."

"I did already. It's the report I was reading when you woke up. From Billy."

"Oh good." She rested her head on her folded arms. "What's the story?"

"Dead girl we found is likely the other girl in the jeep, identity still unknown. Possibly stole your beads from Nikky. Nikky may have been flung out, crawled to the road and found help. Had amnesia for a month or so and made her way back home. That's not too clear."

Amanda exclaimed. "Home? To her mother?"

"Yep. In fact, according to Billy, she returned shortly after her 'burial'." He narrowed his eyes. "Her people came to negotiate for the civil suit while Nikky was home sleeping."

Amanda covered her mouth to stop from shouting. "Does Barrister Ilupo know this?"

"Billy says he denied knowledge. Felt like a real fool." CJ laughed. "Her family never knew about those videos. Never imagined they existed."

"Underestimated your expertise, too." Amanda yawned again. "I wonder what they'll go home to discuss with her?"

CJ chuckled. "That will make interesting news. Remind me to ask Billy to do a follow-up."

Amanda scoffed. "Poor Barrister Ilupo."

"Yeah. The man will avoid any case with my name near it in future."

"That's so—" Amanda closed her eyes. She just wanted to keep sleeping.

****

By evening, Amanda had thrown up the chicken and chips and was running temperature. She shivered so much goosebumps showed on her body, yet her body heat could roast meat. The following morning when she wasn't any better, CJ took her to Kemi's clinic.

"We need to do some tests," Kemi said after taking her vitals. "You said you just returned today?"

"Yesterday." CJ breathed hard. "I mean, she was fine one second. As soon as she ate her mum's food, nothing has stayed down. She thinks it's food poisoning."

"It's possible." Kemi looked at Amanda who lay on the examination table in the office. "I'll have you take her to a lab." She returned to her desk and wrote on a piece of paper. "She'll have to do these tests."

CJ took the paper she gave. "What do you think it is?"

Kemi shrugged. "Pregnancy is first on my list because she just got married." She returned to Amanda's side and smoothed back her hair. "When was your last period?"

Amanda turned her face away. "I...It's not...I don't. I don't know."

Kemi sighed. "I'll give eighty percent she's pregnant." She winked at CJ. "Bad boy, you didn't let her breathe, right."

CJ's brows remained furrowed. "She's never been sick. Like this."

"Don't worry. Take her to get those tests done. I won't suggest she takes any medication for now. By evening I should have the result and we can proceed from there."

CJ gripped his scalp. "Okay, thanks."

"I'll call you as soon as I get the lab result. I've asked that they send it directly to me. And to expedite."

"Thanks a lot, Kemi."

49

—.—

Kemi smiled from ear to ear. "She's pregnant. I think you took in on your wedding day."

Amanda stared into space. CJ took her hand in his and tried to catch her gaze, but her face remained straight.

Kemi shared a glance in between the two. "Am I missing something? Amanda is pregnant!"

"Huh." CJ smirked. "We can't get pregnant."

"Oh." Kemi stared at the sheet in front of her and extended it to CJ. "Look. I ordered several tests. No malaria, no typhoid, no food poisoning. Yes pregnant."

CJ winced. "She doesn't have a womb."

Kemi gasped. "She...dear God!" She stood. "I can order another test in another lab. This looks authentic to me, though, but we can also do a scan—"

Amanda bent her head and wept into her hands. CJ drew her into his arms. "Is there anything you can give her for nausea, better appetite? Nothing stayed today too."

"I won't give any drugs based on this test result." Kemi scratched her head. "Have you been pregnant before, Amanda?"

CJ nodded. "Once. Aborted. It wasn't properly done. They had to take her womb out. She's never menstruated or gotten pregnant again."

Kemi frowned. "Recently?"

"It's been seven years."

Kemi blinked back tears. "You knew and still married her. Oh CJ, you are such a great guy."

CJ growled. "Would I stop loving her because of that?"

Amanda's soft tears grew louder, and she clung to CJ's neck.

"Listen, CJ," Kemi sniffed. "I think this is a miracle and God is sending a message to me, to Yemi to all of us that he is alive and real. And your prayers have been answered."

"We were not praying about it." CJ heaved. "We were just going to adopt."

"Wow." Kemi inhaled noisily. "This is what I'm going to say. Amanda needs to rest a lot, eat whatever she feels like even if she throws it up, and take a lot of fluid. Green tea is great. Ginger tea too, if the smell doesn't nauseate her." She clasped her hands. "We will do a scan in two weeks' time."

"You think I'm pregnant?" Amanda sobbed. "Huh?"

"You are, darling." Kemi hugged her from behind. "You are."

****

"We wanted two years, God gave us two weeks."

Amanda giggled. "Believe me, this son of yours has given nothing. Two months of non-stop attention."

They were home, having a lazy Saturday morning as they'd done since getting married, watching a movie or entertaining guests. CJ pecked the top of her head and for several seconds, both simply watched their son suckle.

"Goodness, see how strong his jaw is."

"Like his father's." She lifted her face and he took possession of her mouth.

"You people will spoil this boy!"

CJ broke off and stared at the front door where Kemi's laughing voice came from as she walked in.

"We didn't know the door wasn't locked," CJ said. "Hello, Kemi."

"You can't be kissing in front of him, do you know that?" Kemi said. "Hello, you two."

"Hi, Sister Kemi." Amanda laughed. "Didn't they say you can do all you like in their presence until they're two years old?"

Kemi exclaimed. "No! One month."

"One month!" CJ gasped. "Then he needs to have his own room immediately."

Kemi laughed. "Miracle Jayamma Okondo! Sweet baby. Don't mind this your *a-love-eh* parents." She tapped his cheeks. "He looks like three months already."

"With the way he sucks, he'll be looking six months by the time he's three." CJ sat on a single couch and Kemi took the space beside Amanda on the sofa. "How's my friend?"

"He's there." Kemi shrugged. "Actually, one other friend of ours wanted to meet you guys. She's been married for eight years and can't conceive. When I told her your story, she asked to meet you. Wants you to talk to her and pray with her."

Amanda moaned. "Wow."

"She just needs to be sincere with God and her husband, or he with her," CJ said. "I think for us, God honoured that. I don't know any formulas, but God just wants us to come as we are and be sincere."

"That's what we've told anyone when we share our story," Amanda said. "What I had feared would become an issue in our marriage became a testimony." She rolled up her eyes to control tears that suddenly sprang to her eyes. "I never imagined God would honour me in such a way."

CJ chuckled. "She cries every time. Says that every time, too."

Amanda sniffed. "My womb grew with my baby."

"It's amazing. I've been in medical practice for over ten years and never seen anything like your case. And usually, it is very very very rare to remove a young girl's womb so the doctor who did it must have been left with no other choice." Kemi shook her head. "Nine months to your wedding day. Just amazing."

CJ nodded. "To the day. The very first time. Baby MJ wasn't joking."

"How do you know it was the first time?" Amanda rolled her eyes. "You couldn't keep your hands off all night, if I remember."

They all laughed.

"Have you guys considered family planning?" Kemi shared a look between the two. "Hmm?"

CJ chuckled. "I want it but Amanda?" He waved at his wife. "Speak for yourself."

Amanda shrugged. For a moment, she stared at MJ as he slept off and his lips drooped off her nipple. She blinked back more tears.

"I just fear another baby won't come if I do it. Like, you know, God has given me a new womb and I'm now trying to block the babies from coming. I don't know." She sniffed. "I don't know."

Kemi patted her hand. "Don't worry, take your time. Whenever you're ready, I'm here. And I'll help you with the best options. Okay?"

CJ winked. "I'm ready to have babies every year."

MJ startled awake and grabbed the nipple again, sucking diligently. The adults laughed.

"A boy on a mission," Kemi said. "He's blessed."

The end

Did you enjoy this book? Please leave a review.
Follow the author to get updates and to connect. Thank you!

Acknowledgments

My profound gratitude to Adeyemi O. Owoade, for his legal review and Dr. Onose Callima-Inino who walked me through the basic ethics in medicine and some details I made quite silly mistakes on. Dr. Chineze Agweye also got my back on this on medical facts. Thanks a lot.

ARE YOU SAVED?

All that is written in this book may not be of much use to you if you haven't yet given your life to Christ. We cannot take difficult decisions unless we have the Righteous and Wise One who is greater than the devil to help and choose for us. The Bible says that "greater is he that is in you, than he that is in the world." (1 John 4:4 King James Version) And "we wrestle not against flesh and blood, but against principalities, against powers, against the rulers of the darkness of this world, against spiritual wickedness in high places." (Ephesians 6:12).

This is why I want to encourage you to take this important decision if you haven't yet given your life to Christ. I took this decision over thirty years ago, and I haven't regretted it even for one day.

Please pray this prayer of faith if you are willing to surrender your life to God:

Lord Jesus, I honour you. I praise you, and I acknowledge you that you are Lord. I know I am a sinner, and I ask that you forgive me all my sins. I want you to be my lord and personal saviour. Wash me clean and give me grace to serve you wholly from now on. Come into my heart to reign supreme. In Jesus' name, I pray. Amen.

PRAISE GOD, YOU ARE BORN AGAIN.

Now that you have prayed this prayer of faith, I admonish you to:

· Get a Bible and read it every day. (Start from the first four books of the New Testament to familiarize yourself more with your new commander in chief, Jesus Christ.)

· Pray every day.

· Attend a Living Church.

· Introduce yourself to the pastor and seek further teaching. (You can join the foundation class and activity group in church. You are, hence, making yourself available to work for God.)

· Tell others about your salvation.

May God help you in Jesus' name. Amen.

The Nigerian Child: My Vision

Then the LORD answered me and said: "Write the vision and make it plain on tablets, that he may run who reads it." Hab. 2:2

More than before, it's time for the well-to-do to cater for the less-privileged. Over the past few years, the Lord has laid this burden for The Nigerian Child on my heart, and I believe it's time to spread the vision. I have a desire to help and to instigate help for The Nigerian Child. There are currently five areas of help I have been able to identify.

1. The Market-school Project: This vision is aimed at eradicating street and market hawking in the long run. The strategy is to erect schools in market places where children hawking can take a few hours out to learn and then go back to their jobs. It is a long-term project and a highly capital intensive one.

2. The Bread and Milk Project: Bread and milk will be given in the morning to children trekking to school just before school resumes. It can be done once a month, once a week, or every day

or as rampantly as the provision is available. It is not very capital intensive, and as little as N50 or $0.35 USD can feed a child with bread and warm milk.

3. The Umbrella Project: This will help alleviate the suffering of children who hawk on the streets (while we work toward eradicating hawking on our streets) by providing umbrellas, especially during the rainy season. The umbrellas can also be useful during the scorching hot weathers. Umbrellas of different sizes will be given depending on the size of the child. Prices of umbrellas range from N350.00 to N500.00 or $2.50 to $3.50 USD.

4. The Sort-a-child Project: This is aimed at helping at least a child in whatever capacity you can. It can be by paying a sick child's hospital bills, buying food and clothing for a child, or paying a child's school fees. It can be as long as a lifetime commitment or a onetime affair.

5. The Student Care Project: This is for secondary and tertiary students who can't afford their school fees. The idea is to help through the bob-a-job initiative.

The Nigerian Child vision is not another nongovernmental, money-spinning organisation. It is service to God and provision for The Nigerian Child. It can be done privately or corporately. The important thing is to help a Nigerian child.

I beg to challenge every church in Nigeria to adopt the sort-a-child project or as the Lord lay it on our hearts.

HELP!
Signed,

- THE NIGERIAN CHILD

- THE NIGERIAN CHILD

Also an Inspired Romance:
Pepper

Other books by the author:
Sister Minister
Strength of Character (Devotional & Workbook for Sister
Minister)
52 ways to provoke God (Devotional)
The devil lied

True dream series:
Dumped
Your wish is mine
Even the lawful captive
He taketh the first
The other sister
What's good for the goose
Shattered
Scattered
Iyke's revenge

Ìka

Battered

Love come by

Novels:

Scent of water

Frail flesh

The days after that night

Tisha

Way of the unfaithful

Foreverland: A Cinderella story

Under a red delta sun

Blue dawn

Wisdom series:

Wisdom for Men

Wisdom for Pastors

Wisdom for Pastors' Wives

Wisdom for Women

Wisdom for Singles

Wisdom for Staying Married

Wisdom for Newlyweds

Issues of life series (Co-authored with Afolarin Ogúnyinka):

Somebody help! She loves my husband

Somebody help! He loves my wife

Somebody help! I'm in love

Some God Use, Some Use God

Revelation series:

Choice